POKER SLAVES

Paige Bond

Copyright © 2021 Paige Bond

All rights reserved

The characters and events portrayed in this book are
fictitious. Any similarity to real persons, living or dead, is
coincidental and not intended by the author.

ISBN-13: 9798706566470

Cover design by: Art Painter
Library of Congress Control Number: 2018675309
Printed in the United States of America

WARNING

This book contains adult content that may be unsuitable for some readers.

This book is intended for adults over 18 and all characters in this story are represented as 18 or over.

ABOUT THE AUTHOR

Follow me on twitter
https://twitter.com/PaigeBondAuthor

Check out my other books on Amazon
https://www.amazon.com/author/paige.bond

Email me - I love getting feedback
paige.bond.author@gmail.com

Ask me a question
https://curiouscat.qa/PaigeBondAuthor

CONTENTS

Title Page

Copyright

Warning

About the Author

Prologue - Friday April 10th   1

Friday March 13th   5

Saturday March 14th   21

Tuesday March 17th   27

Friday March 20th   33

Saturday March 21st   56

Tuesday March 24th   62

Wednesday March 25th   93

Friday March 27th   99

Saturday March 28th   115

Sunday March 29th   132

Monday March 30th   142

Tuesday March 30th   146

Friday April 3rd   152

Saturday April 4th   174

Monday April 6th   176

Wednesday April 8th   182

Thursday April 8th   184

Friday April 10th   185

Saturday April 11th   213

Sunday April 12th   245

Monday April 13th   251

Friday April 17th   254

Afterword   257

About The Author   259

Praise For Author   261

Books By This Author   263

PROLOGUE – FRIDAY APRIL 10TH

Smokes looked at me from across the table. He extended a hand to the ashtray, his eyes never leaving mine and picked up his cigarette. He took a long drag on it, the smoke filling his lungs. He held the smoke in as he replaced the cigarette into the ashtray, then blew the smoke upwards. Behind his left shoulder stood Susie, his girlfriend. She was stripped down to her bra, panties, stockings and suspenders. Finally he spoke.

"Raise you $2,000," Smokes said, pushing $2,000 of chips into the pot.

This was bold, even for him. I could play it safe and fold, then we'd play another round until someone had to re-buy, the price of the re-buy being another item of their girlfriend's clothes.

"All in," I said, pushing whatever I had left into the pot. Jon and Paul inhaled, this was not our normal game.

Smokes smiled and pushed his remaining chips into the pot. If he lost Susie would have to lose her bra (I'd be the winner, I'd get to chose what she lost). Smokes picked up his hole cards and showed his hand. Ace and nine in his hand, which made two pairs with the cards on the table, Aces and nines for him. I tried hard not to smile, I had him. I put my cards down, one on top of the other. I was showing a pair of eights. Smokes made for the money, as his hand touched the pot I separated the cards. With my eight I also had a King, but both were clubs. A flush beats two pair.

"Fuck," said Smokes, "Fuck you man!" His face broke into a broad grin as he said the words. Behind him Susie looked worried.

"Please," she said, "please . . . I, I don't want," her voice trailed out. As the winner the honor was mine. I stood up and walked round the table until I was behind Susie. She was a good girl, she didn't move, her arms folded behind her back. I unhooked her bra and looked across at Willow, my girl, still in her skirt, arms folded the same way. She smiled at me, she wanted to see this as well.

I slipped my hands inside Susie's bra and eased it over her shoulders, down her arms. Smokes moved on his chair to watch. Everyone's eyes were on Susie and my hands. I moved my hands over her shoulders, down her chest. I crossed them over and pushed my hands into her bra.

Susie pushed her head back, closing her eyes. Her protests had died in her mouth. I squeezed her huge breasts inside their container before pushing it down her body. When her tits were free I removed my hands to cheers from Paul and Jay. Mia, Willow and Abi were all smiling (the girls aren't allowed to make any noise). Susie had spoken, she'd be punished for that once her bra was off.

I moved my hands back up her body, taking her tits back into my hands for a second squeeze, then over her shoulders to her arms. I moved them, allowing her bra to fall to the floor, before moving back to my seat.

"You spoke Susie," said Smokes without looking at her, "What should happen now?"

Susie didn't answer for a few seconds, when she spoke she hard tears in her eyes. "I should be punished Sir."

"Yes, yes you should. Walk around the table and offer your tits to everyone for punishment, girls as well."

"Yes Sir," she replied. What else could she say? She set off slowly, trying to delay the inevitable. First stop was with Jon and Mia. Barely able to speak she bent down to Jon.

"Would you like to punish my tits sir?"

"Fuck yes," replied Jon, a massive smile on his face ....

FRIDAY MARCH 13TH

Friday the 13th March, five weeks ago. Unlucky for some, or unlucky for someone.

Paul picked up his beer and took a big swig. "Bored now," he said to the room. I knew what he meant, I was bored too.

We'd all been drinking for a couple of hours with our girlfriends, sat round the dining table. The apartment was a big four bedroomed affair, with separate kitchen, living room, dining room and a tiny box room. It's a great apartment, located centrally near the best bars and clubs. It's not cheap, not by any means. But Smokes is rich, or more to the point, his father is very wealthy and he pays for the apartment for us all. I get to stay in it, as does Paul and John, by virtue of being Smoke's friend. He doesn't charge us anything, otherwise we'd be in some shit hole 15 miles out of town.

Instead we live in town center with a 10 minute walk to work (we all work for the same software company – yes, you guessed it, Smokes' father's firm). It's a sweet deal, we all met at the same college and when we graduated we all applied and were accepted into the same software firm. Not that surprising really, Smokes' father knew us all and liked us and had watched us work at school for four years, he knew what he was getting when he took us on.

It was a Friday night and we should be out down-ing shots in a bar. Shame Susie had forgotten her fake ID and we were stuck in.

Smokes (real name Steve) lit yet another cigarette and made a suggestion.

"Anyone fancy a game of Poker?" He didn't wait for a reply and headed for his room, returning a couple of minutes later with a pack of cards and a box of chips. He opened the box of and counted out $5,000 for each couple.

"The game," he said shuffling the cards, "Is Texas Hold 'em. We've all played before, so let's start. Little blind is $100. Shall we play, say eight rounds and whoever's got the least money at the end forfeits."

"What's the forfeit?" asked Mia.

Smokes looked round – he was the leader of our group but didn't always have the answers. Jon spoke first.

"Strip poker?" he said laughing. A couple of the girls threw things at him and the boys just laughed. Then something happened that surprised me. Willow, my girlfriend, put her beer down, looked round the table and spoke.

"Well, has anyone got any better ideas?"

Silence.

"Right then," said Willow, "No one has any better ideas. All prepared to strip?"

More silence.

"Cool," said Smokes, "what shall we say – one item of clothing on the losing team to be shed?"

Abi looked at Susie who was wearing a sweater and waistcoat over it, "As long as we all start with the same amount of clothing."

We haggled for a bit and ended up agreeing that each girl could wear a pair of panties, bra, shirt, trousers/skirt and socks/pantyhose and shoes. The boys were allowed socks, trousers, shoes, pants and a shirt and jersey, so six items of clothing each. We all went to our rooms to get ready and were back in five minutes.

Smokes shuffled, offered the cut to Jon and dealt out the cards. Paul stuck in a $100 chip and I put in $200. We'd all played before but we're no experts.

We played the eight rounds, taking turns to deal. On the last hand we were all quite nervous, everyone could still win, or lose. The eight hands had taken about 15 minutes – we were playing quite quickly. This was when Smokes showed his skill.

As soon as he looked at his hole cards he folded. I looked at him quizzically.

"Jay mate, I'm ahead $500, if I fold I can't lose." He sat back, high fived Susie and sat back to watch.

The inevitable happened, Willow and I were in last place and so Paul and Jon folded instantly. Bastards. I picked up my beer and took a swig. I looked at Willow.

"Ready?"

Willow shrugged her shoulders, her red hair dancing on her white shirt. She bent down to take off her shoes, then stopped.

"We are playing seriously, aren't we?" she asked. Everyone nodded and so she sat up and slowly unbuttoned her shirt. The whole table, me included were silent as she removed it, revealing her 34DD chest, barely held in by her lacy black bra. She looked at Mia who was staring at her rack.

"Never seen tits this big have you Mia?" Willow asked. Mia blushed, she was tiny with tiny tits, I'd be amazed if they were bigger than 32A. Then Willow looked at me. I smiled, kissed her and removed my sweater.

We played a dozen more rounds, after which Susie and Smokes had removed one item each, both of them selecting their shoes. Jon and Mia had lost three items each, Jon worked out a lot and quickly removed his sweater, shirt and shoes. Mia was more conservative than Willow, she'd taken off her shoes first, followed by her socks and then her skirt, she was pulling down her shirt to cover her panties.

Paul and I had each lost four items of clothing, we were both wearing trousers and underpants. Our girls, Willow and Abi were both in their matching bra and panties sets. I'd stolen more than once glace at Abi, she had a great body. Paul and I were nothing special to look at.

We reset the buy-in with $5,000 Smokes dealt out the cards, the stakes were high now. If I fucked up at cards Willow's bra was coming off. I saw Abi check the clock – she was as nervous as Willow was.

"Shall we make this the last round," asked Abi, "It's getting late."

We all looked at the clock, she was right, we were heading for one in the morning. It would be well after one before we finished another eight hands. Suddenly I was aware of how tired and drunk I was.

"Sounds good," I replied, "but as this is the last round, how about we play until someone is out of money?" Everyone else agreed and we started to play, Paul and I were being very cautious – not for ourselves so much, but if I lost Willow was going to be topless in front of the whole group.

We played a dozen hands before it got serious. I was up a couple of hundred, Smokes was way out in the lead (again) with Jon and Paul down about a thousand each. Paul put in the big blind, up to $1,000 now to try to get to an end before we all fell asleep at the table.

I was dealt a pair of tens, nice. I didn't bet on the first round, no one did and we waited for the flop. Jon was dealing and he turned the cards, a seven, ten and a Jack. This was looking good.

Smokes passed, as did Paul. I didn't think and pushed in $2,000. Jon looked at me and smiled, "Fold," he said, smiling.

Smokes took a long puff on his cigarette before folding. Paul took a long look at me, he was giving nothing away as he pushed $2,000 into the pot. "Call," he said. The stakes were very high now, both of our girls were down to their underwear. I looked at Abi, she was visibly worried. Next I glanced at Willow, she was very cool.

I passed and waited. Jon burnt the top card before dealing an ace. Over to Paul, he hesitated, drank from his beer and stared at his small pile of remaining chips. He pushed the whole pile into the center of the table.

"$1,200, all in," he said.

Everyone round the table was silent. This was going to be it, either Abi or Willow was about to go topless in front of the whole gang, unless I folded. I had three of a kind, it was a strong hand.

I looked longingly at Smoke's cigarette – I don't smoke, but right now I was desperate for a quick hit of nicotine to steady my nerves. Next I studied Paul's face, but I couldn't read him.

"All in," I said. I counted the money on the table, $1,600 and pushed it into the pot. There was no going back.

Jon burned the top card and dealt the river card. Agonizingly slowly he turned it over, a four. No use to me. Paul and I studied each other.

"Time to show your cards Paul," I said. Paul smiled and flipped his cards over. Fuck, an eight and a nine. A straight beats three of a kind. Paul's face broke into a smile. He counted out $400 from the pot and handed it back to me and Willow, taking the rest of the money.

Smokes' deal next. But there was no point, I didn't

have enough for the blind. Paul and Abi relaxed visibility, they weren't going to have to remove any more clothes that night.

"So," said Smokes, "Are you going to deliver Willow?"

We all looked at Willow, she was a fierce redhead and wasn't going to be intimidated by Smokes or anyone else at that table.

"It was my idea Steve," she said, putting her arms behind her back and unhooking her bra. Across the table Smokes put down his beer, "Shit Willow, I didn't think you'd go through with it." Willow smiled at him, she moved the bra down her shoulders, over her elbows and eased her arms out. She put her left arm over her nipple line and pulled the bra away.

Then she held Steve's eyes with hers and slowly, very slowly pulled her arm away, revealing her huge breasts with their creamy white flesh. Willow put her arms by her side and smiled. Everyone in the room was staring at her. She looked at them all, one by one before putting a hand on my shoulder.

"Time for you Jay, remove your jeans."

"Fuck," I said. I stood up and pulled my jeans down, my belly flopping out. The boys all yelled at me to put it away, gross bastard general friendly insults. Willow just stood there smiling.

"Shall I tidy up boys?" she asked, starting to move to pick up the empties and put them in the trash. Everyone was still glued to her as she moved and elegantly tidied the room. When she was done she paused at the door, still just in her panties.

"What do you think, same time next week?" she asked, "and, does anyone want to see the guys naked? Think about it. Come on Jay, bedtime."

I picked our clothes up off the floor and headed for the door. I hoped I was in for a wild night. We walked back to my room, I opened the door and we went in. Willow started giggling, "That was fun Jay, I hope you're OK with it?"

"I'd have been more OK if I'd won."

"But Jay, I doubt any of the others would have gone that far, don't you? Susie's a spoilt rich bitch, there's no way she would have stripped off. But she might now, might she?"

I thought about it, Willow was right. Susie might, now she'd seen another girl semi naked.

"And so," said Willow, draping her arms around my shoulders, "I know you're tired, but I'm horny as hell. And you're going to fuck me."

Drunk and tired as I was how could I say no to a sexy 20 year old with long red hair and huge tits?

Willow pushed me onto the bed and I sat on the corner. She dropped to the floor on all fours and started to shake her hips slowly before crawling across the floor to me. I'd never seen her like this before.

When she was level with me she put her head down to the floor, her hair falling over her head so I couldn't see her face, but I was transfixed. I felt her tongue on my feet, she started at my ankle and dragged her tongue down my foot, before lifting it gently in her hands and she started to suck my toes.

She sucked for a while, I took my cock out of my pants and started to wank myself slowly. I spat into my hand to get some moisture on it, Willow must have heard and she broke off from my foot.

She kissed her way up my legs, alternating from one to the other until she was level with my cock. Her eyes met mine and she smiled at me, before spitting onto my cock.

"Let me do that for you," she said, pushing my hand away and taking my cock into her hand. She wanked me slowly. I watched her for a moment before I lay back on the bed to enjoy the moment. Willow had always been quite conservative before – lights off, me on top, this was new but I was loving her like this.

As I lay down Willow licked one of my balls – shit, she'd never done that before. Oral was an unusual, but welcome, experience and she'd never touched my balls with her tongue. She licked one ball, then the other, all the time wanking me.

Her tongue was replaced by her other hand on my balls when I felt her hot breath – holy fuck, she took one of my balls into her mouth and closed it round, Jesus, this was sensational. Willow sucked on my ball for a moment, I put one of my hands onto her head and pushed her closer – I could feel her breath now on my cock and balls. I was so close to cumming but I wanted to enjoy more of this.

When I released her my ball popped out of her mouth. I'd never experienced anything like that from her. Internally I said 'suck my asshole girl'. Willow lifted my balls and licked from the base of my nuts down. I opened my legs wider and she did it, Willow licked gently round my ass before diving in with her tongue.

"Fuck Willow, fuck, that's incredible," I gasped. She didn't answer, her tongue was inside my ass. I couldn't take it any longer and I started to shout, "I'm cumming Willow, fuck I'm cumming," as hot, thick cum started to spurt out of my cock. Willow didn't move, she kept her tongue in my ass and wanking me slowly. Sticky white cum was shooting out of my cock now and into her thick red hair.

Even when I'd finished cumming she didn't let up, she kept wanking me and fucking me with her tongue. I let her continue, all the time expecting her to stop but she didn't let up. I'd just cum but she wasn't going to let my cock go soft just yet.

Eventually I put my hand on her head and grabbed her hair and pulled her up. She resisted and came up slowly, running her tongue over my balls and up my cock. When her mouth was level with my cock she pulled it down and took my helmet into her mouth.

I propped myself up so I could watch as she started to slide her head up and down my shaft. Willow fixed her eyes on mine as she sucked and wanked my cock slowly. I could feel her breath again, she was breathing quickly and shallowly, I guess she was playing with herself as she sucked my cock.

Eventually she took me out of her mouth and got up onto the bed next to me.

"Fuck me Jay, fuck me like the slut I am," Willow panted. Who was I to refuse?

I rolled over and climbed onto her. Willow put her hands onto the sides of her huge tits and pushed them together and I slid right into her soaking wet pussy. Normally it took ages to get her wet enough to fuck, but not tonight.

I started slowly but it wasn't enough for her.

"Fuck me hard Jay, fuck me fast, fuck me like the slut I am."

I started to buck my hips quickly and Willow took a deep breath in and moaned, "Yes, Jay, that's it. Tell me I'm a slut Jay, fuck your slut."

She had never spoken like this, Willow was usually very reserved.

"You're a slut Willow, you're my slut Willow," I told her

"Fuck yes, I'm a slut," she replied speaking quickly.

"You loved being naked in front of the gang didn't you? You're an exhibitionist slut aren't you?"

"Yes, oh fuck yes," she gasped.

"Jon will be fucking Abi now, but he'll be thinking of you. They'll all be thinking of you. Standing naked in front of them all."

"Jesus yes, oh, oh, Christ I'm cumming, FUCCCK-KKK . . ." Willow was yelling now as she came. I'd never seen her so excited, in the year we'd been together she'd cum once from a vaginal fucking and never this hard.

I slowed down and she yelled again, "Don't stop, don't you fucking stop . . . Christ, I'm going to cum again, shit yes, yes, YES, YESSSSSSSS, Jay fuck YESSSSS". She'd never cum twice, well, not in the same session, not that close together.

Willow let go of her tits and wrapped her arms round me. I stopped thrusting and we lay together kissing before I rolled off her and onto my back. She moved onto her side and put her arm over me and we went to sleep.

SATURDAY
MARCH 14TH

When I woke in the morning Willow was on her side, looking at me. She smiled and purred, "Good morning stud."

"Good morning slut," I replied, half expecting her to hit me. Instead she just laughed a little and smiled.

"I was, wasn't I?" she replied, giggling as she spoke.

"Half naked in front of all those people."

"Well, if you'd played better at cards I wouldn't have been naked, would I?"

"You didn't seem to mind."

Willow blushed, "No, no I didn't. I . . . I liked the attention, having their eyes on me." She stopped speaking for a moment, then her eyes lit up, "Do you think we'll play again?"

"I'm sure the guys will."

She nodded, "And I can convince the girls, I think."

"Even Susie?"

"She will if everyone else does," replied Willow with contempt. They really didn't like each other. "Anyway, I came twice last night, so I owe you one. Fancy a blow job?"

"Err, yes please." I liked the new, assertive Willow. I decided to put my hand on her head and push her down onto my cock. When she was level with my nipples I took her hair in my hand and pulled.

"Ow," she said, looking up at me.

"And this time swallow when I cum." She had never swallowed my cum before, on those rare occasions she sucked my cock she pulled away when I came. Had I pushed my luck too far?

"Sluts swallow," I said, re-enforcing my authority over her.

Willow held my gaze for 10 seconds before replying, "Yes sir, sluts like me swallow."

FUCK!

I pushed her down and she took me back into her mouth, I kept my hand on her head so I could control her as she sucked my cock. Willow held my balls in one of her hands as she lay between my legs. She started slowly, licking my cock up and down, all the time keeping her eyes fixed on my face.

She opened wide and took me into her mouth. I love that sensation, the anticipation and expectation, then the feeling as her warm lips touch my cock and she slid her mouth down – I say she slid her mouth, I had a handful of her hair and was controlling her.

Willow kept her lips in contact with my cock and she sucked gently as I moved her up and down.

"Use your tongue," I ordered her. I couldn't believe that she was allowing me to order and control her like this. Willow obeyed me and I could feel her tongue flicking my shaft and helmet. I put my head back and closed my eyes, it wouldn't be long until I came.

I moved her faster and faster, trying to get more and more of my cock into her mouth. Willow gagged a few times but she stuck to her task. I put my other hand on her head and sped up again, she was moving really quickly now. It wouldn't be long.

"Willow, oh fuck Willow, suck me Willow, I'm . . . I'm going to cum, yes, yes, YESSSS," I yelled as I came. Every time before she'd have pulled away, leaving me to spurt into the bed but I held her head still as I shot spurt after spurt into her welcoming mouth. Even after I'd stopped spurting she didn't pull away.

I held her in place for over a minute before I relaxed my grip and she moved up next to me. She smiled at me, then opened her mouth wide, showing me that she had a mouthful of my cum. Willow closed her mouth and I could see her swallow, then she opened wide again to show me her empty mouth.

We kissed and when I broke it off I looked at her.

"Are you going to swallow from now on Willow?"

She looked at me, "Do you want me to?"

I decided to push my luck again. "I expect you to from now on."

She smiled – what is it about redheads, they look so devilish sometimes when they are smiling, "Then I'm going to swallow your cum from now on."

We kissed again, then I pushed her out of the bed. Willow looked up at me, I slapped her breast, not hard, just playfully.

"Go and get us both a coffee," I ordered her.

Willow stood up and walked to the bedroom door. I loved watching her walk round the room naked, her breasts bouncing as she walked.

"Am I allowed to wear your robe or should I remain naked?" she asked.

I was sorely tempted to tell her to remain naked, but I thought the better of it and allowed her to slip on the robe. As she opened the door it half hid her. She looked at me, half her face hidden behind the door.

"Shall we all play poker again next weekend?"

"Fuck yes Willow," I told her. I'd discuss this next week with the guys. But after sex like that I didn't care who got to see her naked.

TUESDAY
MARCH 17TH

I was in the apartment kitchen reheating my evening meal. Jon and Paul were sat at the table eating when Smokes came in He went straight to the fridge and grabbed a beer and sat down.

"No women?" asked Smokes.

"No," Paul replied, "We're all alone."

"So Jay," asked Smokes, "What was your Friday night like?"

They all laughed – this was the first time all four of us had been alone without any of the girls. I picked up my microwave meal for one and walked to the table. No one spoke as I sat down, peeled back the lid and stirred it. I picked up a forkful of the curry and put it in my mouth. They were all watching me.

"Boys," I replied, trying to sound serious but failing and breaking into a laugh as I spoke, "It was fucking awesome! I though Willow would bottle it and refuse to remove her bra, but man, what a trooper."

"And you were OK with her standing there topless were you?" asked Paul, "I mean, we were all ogling her. Even Abi admitted she couldn't take her eyes off Willow's tits."

"Well, let's put it this way," I replied, "When we got into bed she was like a wild fucking animal. Never see her so adventurous."

This was weird – we just don't discuss things like this in our group. I don't think that boys generally do.

"Question is, how do we top it?" asked Paul.

"Simple," said Jon, "Next time the losing team goes naked."

"Fuck that," said Smokes, "No one, NO ONE wants to see Jay naked. Sorry bud."

He's right. I could lose 20lbs and still be overweight.

"OK then," I said, "We play until one of the girls is naked. And then she has to clean up naked."

There was silence for a moment while they absorbed this.

"Mia will do it," said Jon with certainty.

"You seem very sure of that Jon," I said.

Jon leaned his head back and thought for a moment.

"How long have we known each other?" He looked round the table, "Five years? Six? What I'm about to say goes no further OK? I mean that, you don't tell anyone. Ever. Not even your girlfriends."

We all looked at each other before we agreed, what was he about to say?

"OK, I've been with Mia for almost four years. For the last two she has been my slave."

My fork was half way to my mouth, Paul was drinking his beer and Smokes had the obligatory

Camel in his mouth. I paused and put the fork down, Paul put his beer down, Smokes just left his Camel hanging from the corner of his mouth – he wasn't inhaling, it just hung there. No one spoke or moved. Eventually Paul said what we were all thinking.

"Could you say that again?"

"Mia is my slave. I own her. She does what ever she is told. And if she doesn't, I punish her and then she does it. Look it up guys, it's called BDSM and Mia and I are into it. If I tell her we are playing strip poker and if I lose she will be naked in front of us all then Mia will be naked in front of us all. If I tell her to climb on the table, masturbate, film it and upload it to Pornhub she will. If I tell her she's going to fuck everyone in the apartment, girls included she'll fuck each and every one of you, without question."

We were all exchanging glances.

"I'm serious, Mia is my slave."

"Fuck off," said Paul, eventually.

"Ever wondered why none of us do any housework, yet the place is always clean?" said Jon. He looked round the table at us. "When's the last time one of you washed the dishes? Filled the beer fridge? Cleaned the bathrooms? Anyone?"

There was silence.

"I told Mia it was her responsibility and if she didn't do it, and do it well, she'd get punished. So, she does it all."

I thought about it, shit he was right. I'd not cleaned a damn thing for almost two years, I'd just assumed that one of the other guys did it. We looked at each other, everyone was following the same line of thought. I smiled at Jon with new found respect for my friend and his, well, his slave.

"How the fuck did you manage that?" asked Smokes, finally pulling the camel from his mouth. He asked the question we were all thinking.

"She liked being tied up and it just evolved. After we'd been seeing each other for two years she asked to sign a slave contract and, well, there we are."

"Willow's no slave," I said, "But I think she'd go naked if I lose."

"When," they all replied together.

"Fuck you," I said smiling.

"Abi might," sad Jon thinking, "But one of the other girls would have to get naked first."

Smokes went to pick his Camel out of the ashtray, it had burnt down to the tip so he stubbed it out and tapped another one out of the packet. "I don't think Susie would, not yet anyway."

He lit another one and stood up. He went to the fridge and came back with a six pack.

"OK, here's what we'll do . . . ." he said, opening a cold one.

FRIDAY MARCH 20TH

"So the rules are clear yes?" I said. Everyone nodded.

"And everyone agrees to the rules?" added Willow. She'd been topless last week, this week we were going one step further. We were playing until one of the girls was naked. We all agreed, no one wanted to see any of the guys naked but all of the guys wanted to see the girls. And Willow has told me that she really wanted to see Susie naked to see her humiliated. I wasn't sure that Susie would strip off – Smokes assured me that she would.

"I'll make her," he said with a wink in his eye and with no explanation of how he could be so sure.

I continued. "So, I lost last week," Willow smiled behind me, "So I get to pick the game and get first deal. The game is seven card stud." That shook them all up, they were expecting Texas hold 'em again. Well, I needed to get a competitive advantage. And personally I'd love to play until one of the girls was naked. As long as it wasn't Willow – I wasn't sure she'd keep playing if I kept on losing.

"The starting fund is $5,000 each, rebuy is $5,000 per item of clothing. Ante is $100 to start, increasing by $100 every four rounds. Girls to remain silent at all times – if you speak girls you forfeit an item of clothing. Once down to your underwear you must stand with your arms folded behind your back until the game ends. Naked girl to clean up after the game while we all watch. Ready?"

Everyone nodded again. I picked up the cards, shuffled and passed the deck across for Smokes to cut. Then I dealt, two cards face down to each player. I got a seven and Jack. Not great but could be worse. I wasn't going to bet on that though.

We all passed on the first bet, so at least I got to stay in. The four face up cards were dealt, Ace, Jack and a pair of sevens. This was more like it, a full house on the first round. No one had had such a good hand last week, I did my best to show no emotion as I looked round the other players.

Jon and Smokes both passed before Paul put in $500. I studied him for a moment before I pushed

$1,000 into the pot. Jon folded instantly, then we all looked at Smokes. Living up to his name he picked up his cigarette and filled his lungs with nicotine. He held the smoke in for a few seconds before blowing it all out.

He met my gaze and smiled.

"$4,900, all in," he said. I looked at Susie, she was alarmed at Smoke's recklessness.

"Fuck," said Paul and he folded. I smiled and pushed all my money into the pot.

"Call."

There was nothing to do but deal one more card each. Smokes looked at his next card and smiled. He put them down on the table.

"Ace high flush in spades," he said. I held his gaze and turned over my cards, not even looking at my new card.

"Full house, sevens over Jacks."

Paul and Jon laughed. Smokes didn't react for a moment, then he laughed too. We all looked at Susie. Smokes spoke to her.

"OK Susie, you know the rules. Loose you shoes, or pick something else."

Susie didn't reply, but she stood up and removed her heels. We all admired her ass as she bent over to put them to one side. Susie smiled at us and sat back down, picked up her beer and took a long drink.

As dealer and banker I counted out $5,000 in chips and passed them to Smokes. Willow smiled at me, I'd done well, it was early days but surely better to have won $5,200 on the first round than to have lost $600.

Jon was the next to have to rebuy and I watched Mia move as she sexily removed her shoes. I was still doing well – I'd lost a couple of thousand since the first round but was still well up. Smokes had recovered well but I was still out in the lead.

The game ebbed and flowed for the next hour until I ended up in a face off with Paul. I won again and Abi removed her shoes. I was hoping to see her naked, she had a great body and I loved her exotic Latino skin. This meant that Willow was the only fully clothed girl.

We'd played six times round and the ante was now up to $700. Jon could just make the ante, if he didn't win the next hand he'd have to rebuy in. I decided to watch Mia rather than watch Paul, after all she had more to lose than he did. Smokes knew this as well.

As soon as the hole cards were dealt he bet $500. Paul matched the bet, I had a crap hand but bet anyway. We all looked at Jon.

"I've only got $300 boys," he said, then without looking added, "Take off your shirt Mia."

Mia hesitated, picked up her beer and emptied the bottle. Last week she'd managed to keep her shirt on but she was going to have to reveal a lot more. Slowly she put her hands up to the top button and undid it slowly. We were all watching as she undid button after button. When they were all undone Mia put her hands onto the collar and pulled her shirt open, revealing her bra.

Mia was clearly nervous, she's tiny with seemingly small breasts. She opened her shirt wide, pulling it down her arms. Underneath it Mia was wearing a red push up bra – I was right, she did have small breasts but they suited her frame. Mia also revealed that she was wearing a red suspender belt, the straps hanging down sexily into her skirt.

I picked up my beer and took a swig, then looked at Mia again. I'd missed it at first, she had her belly button pierced with a simple diamond. That was very sexy. Mia sat down and folded her arms over her flat stomach. I counted out another $5,000 for Jon.

Jon took the money and instantly put $1,000 into the pot. The gambling continued and he lost the round. We played for ages, all the girls removing clothes as needed. As we headed towards 10pm it was getting tense.

Mia was by now standing in just her matching red panties and bra. Opposite her Abi was wearing a pure white matching set, showing off her toned abs and pale brown skin. Both girls had their arms folded behind their backs.

Behind me Willow was still seated, she'd lost her shoes, skirt and shirt, but under the rules she could stay seated as she still had her suspenders on. Across from Willow Susie was still seated. She hadn't lost anything more since the first round.

The next few hands were meaningless, small bets going back and forth. Then we got into a big hand.

I folded early, a pair of sevens wasn't going to win anything, but the others all bet big. When they got to the show down Paul and Jon had both gone all in. Smokes had enough that he was safe, or rather Susie was safe, for the next round. But one of Mia or Abi (or both!) was about to lose their bra. The cards were about to be turned.

Smokes had dealt, so Paul showed first. He turned over his three hole cards.

"Straight, ten high," he said with a big smile on his face. I looked at Abi behind him, she was nervous as hell.

"Shit," said Jon, throwing down his cards, "three of a kind."

No one moved. Jon turned to Mia. "Take off your bra Mia."

Would she do it? I knew that Jon had described her as his slave, but I wasn't 100% sure that I believed him. Her arms were already behind her back and we were all looking at Mia. She had big eyes for her small frame and body and they were open wide. Jon looked away from her, towards Paul, opposite him at the table.

"Mia, take off your bra. Now."

Mia took a deep breath, I saw her arms move, then her bra straps loosened over her shoulders – she had unbuckled it. Slowly Mia took her hands out from behind her back and slipped her left hand under the right shoulder strap and pushed it down her arm.

Mia used her left hand to push the bra over her arm, covering her nipple with her hand. She then repeated the moves with her right hand. The bra fell to the floor and Mia covered her small breasts with her hands.

Mia smiled, looked at everyone in turn then revealed her breasts. Fuck me, her belly button wasn't her only piercing, she had metal rings through both of her nipples. Mia moved her hands to the opposite breast and rubbed her nipples, which grew quickly as she rubbed them. We all watched in silence.

Mia smiled at the group then put her arms back behind her back

Paul whooped, "Yes!" I tore my eyes away from Mia's tits and looked at Abi. The relief was written all over her face. Paul moved his hands towards the pot.

"What are you doing Paul?" asked Smokes. Paul paused, "You've not seen my cards yet Paul," Smokes added. We all looked at Smokes. He smiled, he loved being the center of the attention. Guess it came with the money and prestige of being a dot com millionaire's child.

He pushed his three cards forward and fanned them out. Painfully slowly he turned the first one over, a ten. Now he had a pair of tens and the pair of threes on the table. Next he turned over the middle card, a queen. Nothing there, he still had two pair.

The bastard paused and took a drag on his Camel before flipping the final card. Another 10, a full house. I shook my head, he had a flair for both the game and the dramatic. He looked at Paul and smiled.

"My pot Paul."

Paul shook his head, but he was smiling. He turned to Abi.

"Showtime Abi, take your bra off." Abi looked

round the table, she took her arms out from behind her back, she was shaking. Abi slipped the shoulder straps down her arms, then reached behind her back, before putting her arms at her side.

"Please," she said, her voice tailing off into nothing, desperately looking for some support. By the rules of the game she should also lose her panties for speaking, but no one was going to enforce that on her. Not this time anyway, you can't push these things too quickly.

Abi fixed her eyes on Susie first who just smiled an evil smile at her. No support there. Next Abi looked at Mia, who was smiling at her, dressed in just her tiny panties, her pierced breasts on display.

Finally she looked to Willow for support. Willow was having none of it, she'd stood there almost naked last week, why should Abi be let off?

Slowly Abi put her hands up, covering her breasts and unhooked her bra (front fastening – I love that) and she eased it off her tits. Her bra fell open, still hanging off her shoulders, she kept her hands covering her tits. She looked round the table again. Then very slowly she pushed her bra off her shoulders and it slipped down her arms. She moved her arms one by one to allow it to fall to the floor, always keeping her nipples covered. When it was on the floor she stood there in silence, her left arm hiding her modesty. Paul turned to her. His voice was cold.

"Put your hands behind your back Abi."

Abi continued to shake as she pulled her arm away from her tits. Finally we could see them, she had a great pair. She folded her arms behind her back and defiantly looked around the room. I looked behind me, Willow was admiring Abi's rack, that was interesting.

We played on, I was next to have to rebuy, Willow removed her stockings and suspenders without discussion and stood up in her bra and panties.

We played on, my luck had changed and I (or rather Willow) was safe, Paul and Jon were both hemorrhaging chips. The ante was now up to $1,000 and I reckoned that both of them had only just more than that in front of them.

We each put in $1,000 I was right, Jon only had $800 more left. Paul dealt. My hole cards were nothing special and I passed, as did everyone else. Next he dealt four cards face up. That was better – I had a pair of Queens. On the table was a Queen, a

Jack and a pair of 5s.

I was in no rush and passed again. Jon didn't hesitate and pushed all his $800 into the pot. Smokes folded. Paul hesitated and looked at his cards again, always a bad sign. He counted his chips, $900.

"Looks like I have no choice," he said and pushed $900 forward. That was it, either Abi or Mia was about to be fully naked. I surveyed the room as well, there were empty beer bottles, pringles tubs and general untidiness. The rules were clear, the losing girl had to clean the room – on Tuesday we'd decided that this meant not just tidying up the beer bottles, it meant cleaning the room. I guessed it would take her an hour or more.

I folded, there was no point staying in the game.

Jon eyed Paul, "Shall we just turn over our hole cards?"

"Might as well."

Jon flipped his cards. A seven and a five. Three of a kind. Paul did likewise, he had a Jack and an eight. It all depended on their next card. I looked at Abi, she was terrified, fear was written all over her face. I looked at Mia, she didn't seem that bothered, but then Jon was winning.

Paul burned the top card then dealt one face up to Jon. An Ace, meaningless in the context of the game. Everything came down to the next card. He dealt one to himself, face down. Paul picked up one of his hole cards and flipped the face down card. A Jack and Abi was safe, anything else and she would be as naked as the day she was born.

The lucky bastard, it was a Jack. I could hear Abi breathe out, how long had she been holding her breath. Mia was going to have to strip.

Jon shook his head and laughed. He rubbed his ear with a finger and swigged from his beer.

"OK Mia, time to show the guys the rest of your piercings."

The rest of her piercings . . . the rest of her . . .

Mia didn't speak, she unfolded her arms and put her index fingers into her panties and pushed them down, over her hips, down her short legs. She bent at the waist as she pushed them down her calves before stepping out of the lacy material.

Mia kicked them away and straightened up before folding her arms back behind her back. Jon was the only person not looking at her hairless body. I looked at Susie, she had her eyes fixed on Mia's pussy.

"Turn around Mia," he ordered her, "Bend over and pull your ass cheeks apart. Show them your pussy – and your tattoo."

Mia did as she was told, she turned round, bent over. She opened her legs wide and put her hands onto her ass and pulled her cheeks apart. I don't think anyone was breathing. Her outer labia were pieced with two simple studs in each. Her clit had a ring in it, I'd never seen anything like it in real life.

And shit, on her left ass cheek was a tattoo of a naked woman, on her knees with her arms outstretched. I was getting hard just looking at her. I looked at Willow, she was transfixed looking at Mia.

Mia stayed like that for five minutes before Jon allowed her to straighten up. When she did he ordered her to tidy up. Abi took that as a sign and bent to pick up her bra.

"No Abi," said Paul, "We lost, that stays off until we go to bed. And we're not doing that until this room is tidy." He pulled back his chair and told Abi to sit on his knee. She hesitated and Paul spoke to her. "Or sit on Jay's knee, your choice."

Deciding Paul had made the best offer she sat on his knee and put her arm around him. Paul put one of his hands onto her breast. She made to remove his hands a few times before accepting what was happening and left them. Susie sat on Smokes and Willow sat on me. We sat and talked (girls joining in) while Mia cleaned and tidied.

When my beer was empty I just shouted at Mia, "Mia, get me a beer. And anyone else want one?"

Poor Mia, she had to struggle with six beers, Susie said she'd had enough to drink. We sat and chatted, watching and admiring the half naked and totally naked girls as we talked and Mia worked.

It took Mia just under an hour to do everything apart from the vacuuming. When she came in with the machine she plugged it in and started to vacuum. We all stood up and headed to bed. As Smokes walked past he slapped Mia on her ass. Paul did the same, as did I. What surprised me was Willow also gave her a hard slap as she walked past and held her hand there for a good few seconds after she'd slapped Mia. I smiled, I was in for a good night.

When Jon and Mia left the room the rest of us left too. As soon as my room door shut Willow removed the rest of her clothes and dropped to the floor. I was sat on the edge of the bed and she took my cock into her mouth and sucked till I was hard. When I was fully erect she popped me out of her mouth and started to talk to me.

"Did you see Mia," she asked, wrapping her hand round my cock and starting to wank me slowly, "Did you see her piercings and tattoos?"

"Of course," I replied, "She looked hot."

"And that tattoo . . . sexy . . . sexy . . . Fuck me Jay, fuck me now."

"Get on the floor," I told her. Willow pushed herself back and lay on her back.

"No," I told her, "Get on your hands on knees." Willow rolled over and raised herself up as I'd told her. We'd never fucked like this before. She separated her knees and pushed back, her pussy exposed. I slid off the bed and put my hands on her hips.

Willow leaned on her left arm and pushed her right arm between her legs and grabbed my cock. She wanked me slowly, pulling my cock towards her hole. I gasped as she lined up my helmet with her pussy and she pulled me in.

"Put your head on the floor Willow," I ordered her.

Willow didn't speak, she lowered her head down, her shoulders touching the carpet. She turned her head to one side and opened her mouth, groaning as I fucked her

To get a better hold of her I let go of her hips and grabbed her shoulders, pulling my hands down her arms, over her elbows towards her wrists. When I had them in my hands I pulled them hard, forcing her back further onto my cock. Willow winced in pain as I pulled, but she didn't ask me to stop.

Next I pulled her wrists into the small of her back and crossed them, holding both of her delicate thin wrists in my left hand. I crushed the bones together, again Willow gasped but she didn't ask me to stop.

To complete my dominance over her I leaned forward and grabbed a handful of her long red hair in my right hand and pulled back firmly. Willow's neck snapped back, her chin now on the floor and I kept fucking her, she was unable to move in the position she was in. If she asked me to stop I would, but she said nothing and just assumed the position of my fuck toy.

I kept fucking her in that dominant/submissive pose. Poor Willow was groaning and moaning – half in pleasure, half in pain.

"Fuck me Jay, do what you want with me, enjoy yourself," she gasped through her panting, "Don't think about me." Who could refuse such an offer?

I started to pant, I was getting close, Willow was being so submissive it was one hell of a turn on. "I'm going to cum in you Willow, fuck I'm going to cum."

"Yes, yes, fuck me Jay, fuck me hard."

I let go of her wrists, I wanted to play with one of her tits. Good girl, she didn't move her arms from where I left them. I reached under her and grabbed one of her huge tits, my fingers seeking her nipple. When I found it I took it between my finger and thumb and squeezed hard.

"Aaarrrrg," screamed Willow, "Hurt me more, really hurt me."

Fuck, she was turning me on. I squeezed harder and she cried out again. I was going to cum in her.

"I'm cumming Willow . . . YESSSSSSS." I stopped fucking her, my cock buried in her pussy. I pulled harder on her hair and she cried out again. This was incredible.

When I stopped cumming I still didn't let up and I held her in place for another minute before I released her. I pulled out of her and sat back up on the end of the bed. Willow didn't move for a moment. When she did she got back onto all fours and crawled away from me to the end of the bedroom.

When she reached the wall she turned round and looked up at me, then crawled back, flexing her body, her ass wiggling as she moved. When she was level with me she got onto her knees and kissed my cock, taking it into her mouth. She sucked it straight down.

"Do you like the taste of your pussy?"

"Mmmmmm," she hummed as she sucked, she popped it out of her mouth and spoke softly, "I love the taste of my pussy on your cock."

This was unexpected, I'd expected her to say no but that she wanted to please me. I was drunk and pushed my luck.

"Maybe one day you'd like to suck another girls juices off my cock."

Shit, she looked up at me. I'd meant to just think that.

"I would if you wanted me to. Or maybe I could just suck her pussy directly?"

She didn't wait for an answer and took me back into her mouth and sucked up and down. I could see her hand moving between her legs as she played with her clit. What the hell.

"Keep sucking my cock Willow, imagine you're sucking Mia's pussy juice off my cock."

Willow moaned.

"You had to kneel at the end of the room while

I fucked her. You watched her bouncing up and down on my cock. She's got a tiny body, her cunt is so tight. I came in her, after you clean my cock you'll have to eat my cum from her cunt."

"Fuck, I'm cumming Jay . . . oh fuck, please . . . PLEASE . . . . I'm cumming . . . . YESSSSSSSS", she yelled, my cock coming out of her mouth as she spoke, then straight back in to suck again

I'd never heard Willow that loud as she came, my cock still buried in her face. I could feel her mouth moving, she was doing well not to bite me. She held me there for almost 30 seconds as she came. I put my hands on her head to help hold her in place.

When she tried to pull her head off I held her in place. She started to struggle, putting her hands onto my legs and pushing.

"No Willow," I told her – I could feel my cock pulsing as I controlled her – "Put your arms behind your back." She didn't move so I re-enforced the command, "Do it, NOW".

Willow did as she was told. I held her for another 10 seconds before releasing her. She pulled straight off my cock and started to breathe quickly, replenishing the oxygen in her system.

She looked up at me, she was kneeling on the floor, her legs apart, arms folded behind her back. I thought of Mia, the slave girl. Was this how she knelt before Jon? Could I make her kneel before me like this? Could I make her my slave?

I ran my fingers through her hair. I patted her head and when I tried to pull my hand back she grabbed my thumb in her mouth and she sucked it. Our eyes met and I spoke to her.

"Good girl," I said. Shit, that was so demeaning to her.

"Thank you," she replied, "glad I pleased you."

I pulled my thumb out of her mouth and stood up. "I'm going to the bathroom, stay there," I told her. Willow just nodded.

I came back about 10 minutes later, she was exactly where I had left her. I allowed her to use the bathroom, when she came back I was in bed. Willow got in next to me and put her head on my chest. I ran my fingers through her hair again.

"Sleep well," I told her.

"You too," she replied and we went to sleep,

wrapped in each other's arms.

SATURDAY
MARCH 21ST

I woke in the morning with the light just creeping round the drapes (my room faces just about East). First thing I noticed was Willow snuggling up to me, her breasts on my chest, her long red hair half covering me. Second thing, shit my head hurt. Not so much one beer too many last night as three too many. I pushed Willow to one side and she rolled over, then I limped out of bed without waking her, slipped on my robe and left my room.

Next was a quick visit to the bathroom before entering the kitchen. It was still early, I checked my watch, just before seven am. I needed coffee and I could smell it. First, a glass of water. I downed that and instantly felt worse, before I found the paracetamol and took two with another glass of water. I'd start to feel better soon. I could still smell the coffee. I turned round, there was a pot on the go. I took a cup out and poured myself one.

Holding my cup I moved from the kitchen table, sat down and poured the hot black liquid down my throat. Ah, that felt a little better, I could feel my headache recede a little. Next stop would be the shower, five minutes under the steam and I'd be almost back to normal. Almost.

After my shower I did feel better. Wrapped in a towel I got two cups of coffee from the percolator and went back to my room. I kicked open the door with my foot and went in as quietly as I could, I hoped Willow would still be asleep.

I turned as I went into my room, I put the coffee down on the desk and closed the door with my hands, took off my robe and hung it on the door then turned to see if she was awake. Holy fuck she was awake, Willow was out of the bed and kneeling on the floor, like she had been the previous night, legs wide apart, her smooth, hairless pussy on display, arms at her side, hands on her legs, head down. I looked at her.

"Coffee?" I asked.

"Yes please and thank you," she replied. Willow didn't move so I bent down and put the cup between her legs. She used her right hand and picked it up, then started to drink. I could feel my cock twitch, as if it had a life of it's own as she knelt submissively in front of me. I sipped on my coffee, staring at her full chest. Neither of us spoke. When I drunk half my mug I spoke to her.

"Have you been like that for long?"

"Since you got out of bed," she replied, "I can't see a clock, I don't know how long I've been waiting for you to come back." I looked, shit, almost 25 minutes. I didn't know what to say, so I said nothing and drank up. When I finished I grabbed the desk chair and pulled it between her legs, then sat on it. Willow took her last mouthful and looked up at me. My cock had a life of it's own now, she smiled at me and put her hands on my thighs, under the towel and slid them up. The towel came undone and she leaned in, extending her tongue and licked my cock from the base to the tip.

She lined her mouth up with my shaft and took it gently into her willing mouth. For a girl that had rarely sucked my cock until three weeks ago this still felt magical. I gasped as she took me into her mouth, shit she still had a mouthful of warm coffee and the heat on my cock felt incredible – I'd never experienced anything like that before. I didn't speak, just relaxed back on the chair as she used her mouth, up and down, up and down, teasing me with her tongue. The coffee was cooling, the sensation wasn't entirely unpleasant but I was glad when she took a break and swallowed it.

Up and down she worked, legs never moving, never complaining. The pain in her legs must have been considerable but she stuck to her task. I leaned in and took hold of her ample beasts and squeezed, normally I'd caress and be gentle with them, today I wanted her to feel a little pain. Willow whined a little when I crushed her nipples in my fingers, but she didn't stop. Instead she started to wank the base of my cock, timing her strokes to match her mouth.

My balls were drenched in her spit, she was doing a good job of choking herself and gagging, so I was covered in her saliva. I was getting close, my cock trembling in her mouth as she worked up and down. I squeezed her nipples hard, sinking my nails into her sensitive skin and she half cried out, the sound of her in pain pushed me over the edge and I started to cum, pumping load after load into her mouth. As expected now, when I finished cumming she sat back and swallowed my cum, then smiled up at me.

"Can I get you another drink Jay?"

"Yes please Willow," I replied. I watched as she pushed back and brought her knees together, then she put her hands on my knees to raise herself up, her face had indications of pain as she moved, she'd been kneeling like that for over 30 minutes and I guess she was pretty stiff. When she was up-right she bent her legs once or twice before mov-ing to the door.

At the door she took my robe off the hook. I de-cided to see how far I could push my luck with her.

"Put that back," I ordered Willow as I turned to face her. She looked at me and smiled to herself, then hung it back on the door.

"Shall I go naked Jay?"

I smiled. "Yes." It was a good risk, normally we're the first up on a Saturday and that's normally gone 10. It was seven forty-five and I'd be amazed if anyone else was up. She smiled at me and nodded, then picked up the coffee cups, opened the door and went through it. I stood up, wiped her saliva off my cock and got into bed. Willow was soon back and she got into bed with me.

"That was pretty thrilling," she said as she sipped her refill, "I kept thinking I'd get caught."

"Well," I replied, "It's not like they've never seen

you naked before is it?" Willow laughed and hit me with a pillow.

"The difference is that this time I did it because you ordered me to. I'd do anything you order me to."

I sat back and sipped my coffee. I needed to think about what she'd just said. I needed to talk to Jon about him and Mia. How should I proceed?

TUESDAY
MARCH 24TH

I was pretty sure that Jon and I were alone in the apartment, Smokes and Paul had said they'd see us later when they slipped out. We were going to meet them in a bar. I needed to talk to him about Willow. Jon is my best friend, we'd roomed together in our first year at college. He was the only one I could open up to. And, given that Mia was his slave, he was probably the only one that would have any experience to offer.

"Jon," I said, my voice low and quiet to show I was being serious, "Jon, I need to talk to you."

Jon looked at me, I could almost see his brain working out that I wasn't about to ask for $10.

"Sure man, let me grab a couple of beers and we can talk." He'd worked out that this was something serious. We sat at the kitchen table and he opened the beers, gave me one. We clinked then downed a couple of inches. I didn't know where to start.

"Is this going to take all night Jay – we're supposed to be shooting pool with Steve and Paul."

I blushed, I was avoiding speaking. "I . . . I need to talk to you about Willow."

"Shit, is she pregnant?"

"No, at least I don't think so."

"Fuck, is she leaving you?"

"No, not that either." I drank a bit more.

"Jay, if I have to play 20 questions to get out of you what's wrong we could be here all night."

He was right. I picked up my beer and downed it, the cold liquid soothing my suddenly parched throat. I could feel it starting to work in my stomach, the instant hit of alcohol warming me and bringing me the confidence to speak.

"I . . . I . . . look, the last couple of nights Willow has been, how shall I put this, she's been, she's been more than a little submissive to me." There, I'd said it. It was out in the open.

Jon wiped his face with his hand, then picked up his beer and drank some.

"And you wanted to talk to me as that's how Mia and I are?" He asked, I just nodded. Jon smiled at me then stood up. "Let me get you another beer Jay." He walked to the fridge and came back, opened one and passed it to me.

"How submissive has she been?"

I told him about her wanting to be held down, kneeling before me and going to the kitchen, naked, to get coffee, just because I told her to. When I finished speaking he looked at me.

"One second Jay," he said. He took out his phone and typed a quick message, then looked back at me.

"And how do you feel about this?"

"I'm not sure," I replied, "Don't get me wrong, having her so submissive and suddenly becoming so adventurous in bed is fantastic. I mean, who wouldn't want a hot girl obeying your orders?"

Jon nodded, drank a little then spoke to me more seriously. "How far do you want to take it?"

"I don't know, I mean, I don't know how far I could."

"Jay, the one of the hardest parts of owning Mia is having to think for two people. You're not just in command of yourself, you have to think for her as well. But that's not the hardest. The hardest is when she fucks up, you have to punish her."

My eyes opened wide as he said that. "Pardon?"

Jon laughed, "When Mia fucks up I punish her. I inflict pain on her as a reminder of how she's fucked up. Could you bring yourself to hurt Willow? Not just slap her a little, I mean really hurt her, hurt her so that she'll still have the marks on her a few days later?"

I thought about this. "I don't know."

"Well," he said, "If you can't, you're never going to make it as a slave owner. Mate, it sounds to me like Willow might want to be a slave, or at least she's becoming more and more submissive and that will lead her to being a slave. But if you're not prepared to go the other way and become her master, you're going to lose her to someone who will.

Shit, I hadn't thought of it like that.

"You need to know what your limits are Jay." Jon winked at me and raised his voice. "Get in here".

I looked at the door, shit I'd thought we were alone in the apartment. Mia crawled into the kitchen, she was naked. On her neck was a leather collar with a leash hanging down from it. Mia looked up at me and blushed, but crawled to Jon and offered him her leash. I was transfixed, I couldn't speak as I watched them. Mia raised herself up onto her knees, opened them wide and folded her arms behind her back, her head down.

Jon thrust out his hand, the one holding Mia's leash and pushed the loop into my hand, then he stood up. Jon looked at the clock and spoke to Mia.

"Mia, Jay is aware of our relationship. I'm going out now to meet the boys and I'll cover for you Jay. I won't be back before 11. When I do, I expect to find you in my room Mia, alone. Until then I give you to Jay for the evening. You will never speak of what the two of you do. Period. Even if I ask or order you, you must never reveal what goes on between you. Understand?"

"Yes Master," she replied.

"And Jay, do what you like with her. Just one thing, make sure you whip her hard, several times. Whip her so she screams in pain, just to prove to yourself that you can do it. No objections to that have you Mia?"

"None Master," she said.

Jon smiled at me. "Because if you can't do that, it doesn't matter how submissive Willow might be, you'll never cut it as her owner. Enjoy your evening with a totally obedient slave girl Jay."

He was almost at the door when I found my voice.

"What, wait Jon." He paused then looked at me. "What can I do with her?"

"Anything. Fuck her if you want, make her drink your piss. Parade her naked round the town. Whatever you want. Mia has no limits, do you slave?"

Mia blushed with embarrassment. "No Master,

your slave has no limits."

"Two more things Jay. First, don't cause any permanent damage to her, no broken bones etc. Bruises, whip marks are fine. Second, give her marks out of 10. See ya Jay, have fun!" and with that he was gone.

I didn't move or speak for a full five minutes, neither did Mia, she just stayed where she was, head down, waiting on my orders. I really wasn't sure of myself. Eventually I found my tongue and spoke to Mia.

"So Mia, you'll obey my every order?"

"Yes sir," she replied, "My master's orders were clear."

"And you'll never tell anyone what goes on for the next," I checked the clock, "three hours or so?"

"No sir, what goes on between us stays between us."

Did I feel guilty that I was about to cheat on Willow? A little, yes. I tried to justify myself, to make excuses. It wasn't really cheating, was it – more seeing if I could be the man that I thought Willow wanted me to be, I was learning how to handle a slave, I was just playing. But the truth is I was cheating on her. If she 'experimented' with Jon I'd be mighty pissed, but hey, Mia was naked, willing to serve and had promised to never discuss the next few hours with anyone. I'd be a fool not to take advantage.

"Suck my cock Mia."

Mia smiled, "My pleasure sir." She reached up, undid my trousers and took my semi hard cock into her tiny mouth. I gasped, Willow started slowly, not so with Mia. She took me straight down and sucked hard, her lips touching my skin, her nose full of my pubes. I took my eyes off her and looked round, suddenly nervous. Willow had a key for the apartment.

I was about to ask Mia to stop, to pause for a moment, but surely that's not the right way to treat a willing slave girl? Instead I put my hand on the side of her head raised it up, grabbing a handful of her long dark hair. I twisted it into a bunch and pushed her down, holding her in place for a few seconds, before yanking her hair, pulling her upwards. I'd never treat Willow like this. Mia looked at me, I expected her to complain at the way I'd just treated her. She surprised me.

"I'm sorry if I'm doing it wrong sir," Mia said, sounding nervous, "Please tell me how you like your cock sucked or punish me if you really hated it sir."

Wow! How submissive was Mia? "No, nothing wrong. Just go to the door and put the chain on. I don't want to be disturbed."

Mia smiled, "I think that's a good idea sir." I started to move and she spoke again, "Let me do it sir, why have a dog and bark yourself?" Why indeed. I watched her crawl to the door, she was very sexy, putting one leg in front of the other, showing me her pussy and ass. At the door she paused and looked at me, smiling again. Clearly she was loving the attention. Shit, her cunt was glistening, she was soaking wet.

Mia moved quickly and was soon back in front of me. She quickly took me back into her mouth and started to suck. Mia's tiny, her whole frame is tiny and she had to open her mouth wide to get my cock in. Fuck, I put my hand on her throat and I could feel my cock moving in and out as she sucked me up and down. I'd never experienced anything like that, having my shaft actually in a girl's throat. I wanted a better view.

Again, I hauled her off and pulled her to her feet, she didn't resist as I walked her round the table, I pulled back on her hair and she cried out in pain, I was forcing her head upwards so Mia had to stare at the ceiling, her neck bent back as far as it would go. The table was clear, I held her at one side while I walked to the other, body away from the table, head held back at a painful angle.

Once I was on the other side of the table I pulled her down by her hair, her back bending, down onto the table so she was lying on her back. Mia was well trained, she shuffled backwards until her neck was just off the edge of the table, her back and ass on it. She leaned her head back and opened her mouth wide, legs as well. I couldn't resist and thrust my cock back into her head, sinking it all the way in, taking it slowly so I could watch as her throat bulged and pushed against the collar on her neck.

I took hold of the leash, not that I needed it to control her, I liked the feel of control it gave me over her. I slowly fucked her throat, each time pulling all the way out of her mouth, just giving her a few seconds to breathe, before pushing back down her throat. Every time I pulled out some saliva came with my cock and I loved watching it drip off and down her face, over her cheeks and eyes, making her makeup run. Mia's eyes were wet, she wasn't crying but moisture was running from the corners. Fuck she looked hot.

I put hand hands onto her small tits, I took the bars of her nipple piercings and pulled on them, lifting her breasts upwards, causing her pain. There was no doubt in my mind, I was enjoying using her and inflicting pain on her. Maybe I could make it as an owner?

Mia's hands were at her sides, when Willow sucked my cock she usually played with herself, Mia wasn't allowing herself any such pleasure. I released my grip on the metal bar and used the leather handle of her leash to whip her cunt. I timed it so my cock was at it's maximum depth in her throat when I lashed her. Each time her back lifted and she tensed her hands, she cried a little I think, it was fucking hard to work out the noises she was making but she didn't resist. Fuck, I had to train Willow like this.

I kept this up for a few minutes, when I could feel myself close to cumming I pulled out and started to wank myself, shooting thick loads of cum over her face, watching it drip into her nose and eyes. I screamed in delight, it felt incredible to know that she was there for my pleasure. Mia was superb, even as my cum dripped into her eyes she kept them wide open, allowing it to fill her eyes before it continued to drip down to her forehead.

I pushed my cock back into her mouth to clean it, Mia reached behind me and grabbed my ass, pulling me even deeper into her throat. I allowed her to clean me for a few minutes before I pulled out, despite her best efforts my cock was softening. When I pulled out I looked at her, her face was a mess with saliva and cum.

"Clean yourself up slut," I said, surprising myself with my choice of words.

Mia put her hands onto her face, using her fingers to pull the disgusting mixture of spit and cum to her mouth then sucked her fingers clean, swallowing it all, making appreciative noises as she swallowed my cum. I couldn't take my eyes off the scene in front of me.

When she'd swallowed it all Mia continued to lick her hands and fingers, shit I could feel my cock twinging and starting to get hard again. I was going to cum again that night I knew. I was about to help Mia off the table when I changed my mind, instead I just grabbed her hair and pulled her across the table, dragging her. When her ass came over the edge of the table she bent in half and fell to the floor, Mia cried in pain, for a couple of seconds I was holding her by her hair.

I started to walk to the living room, dragging poor Mia by her hair, her ass on the floor. She didn't weigh much and was easy to drag, Mia grunted a few times but she didn't resist. I had an idea of something I'd always wanted to try but never dared ask any girl. Mia wouldn't say no, I knew that based on what she'd already done. Actually I had several ideas I wanted to try with her . . . . I just needed time to plan.

As soon as we were in the living room I sat down on my favorite chair. I released my grip on Mia and she fell onto her back, before twisting over and getting back into her submissive pose, legs wide apart kneeling at my feet.

"Take my shoes off Mia, rub my feet."

"Yes sir," she replied and started to obey. She quickly removed my shoes and socks and started to rub my feet, her hands were soft and gentle and she worked hard. Without asking she started to suck my toes – girls had done this to me before but this was different. My being fully clothed and her naked made the scene far more erotic. I left her to work on me while I planned out what we were going to do next. In the back of my mind were Jon's words – at some point I had to punish Mia, though if she stayed this submissive I'd struggle to find any reason to punish her. I picked up the remote and flicked the TV on, ignoring Mia.

When I was bored of her rubbing my feet I ordered her to get on all fours which she quickly did. I raised my legs up and put them into the small of her back and settled down to watch the last three innings of the game. Mia stayed almost motionless throughout, head down.

As soon as the game was finished I put my first idea into action. I took my legs off her back and stood up, I half expected Mia to move but she stayed exactly where I was. I couldn't resist and I climbed onto her, sitting on her back. Mia groaned, I probably weighed twice as much as she did but I'd fantasized about this situation for years, ever since watching it in a porno.

Slowly I raised my legs up until Mia was carrying my entire weight. I wrapped my legs under her stomach, with my left hand I grabbed her hair and pulled it tight, forcing her head up once again. With my right hand I slapped her ass.

"Walk on Mia," I ordered her. Mia raised her right hand and pushed it about eight inches forward, then moved her left leg. Slowly we walked across the living room floor, heading to the door.

"Sir," said Mia. Shit, was she going to object? That would give me reason to punish her, "Sir, if you want to ride me would you like me to get my bit gag and riding crop?"

"Fuck yes Mia," I replied, barely able to contain my enthusiasm for this. I wasn't really sure what a bit gag was but I wanted to find out. I rode Mia to the door to Jon's room where I dismounted and Mia crawled in. She was back in less than two minutes, holding a rubberized tube, about six inches long and an inch in diameter. On each end was a steel ring, a couple of inches in diameter with leather straps attached and a leather belt. She was also carrying a riding crop. Mia got onto her knees and opened her legs, then offered the items to me.

"Sir, the gag goes in my mouth and forces my jaws open, you fasten the belt behind my head to hold it in place. You can then control me with the reins and crop me if you feel like it, or want to enforce an order or punish me if I displease you sir."

Who was I to say no? I took the gag off Mia and she opened her mouth wide, so I pushed it between her teeth, as far back as I could. Mia bit down on it to hold it in place while I reached behind her head and fastened the belt. I could see from looking at it that Jon had 2 holes on the belt that had been used more frequently. Fuck it, I selected the tighter one. Mia gasped as I fastened it in place, I could feel her mouth open wider and the gag moved back a quarter inch or so.

I moved back to look at her, Mia looked stunning with her mouth forced open. The only down side of this I guess was I couldn't fuck her mouth. Ah well, I could always take it out again later. I took the reins and pulled her down onto all fours before climbing back onto her back. I held the reins in my left hand and the crop in my right. I didn't speak, just reached behind myself and lashed her exposed butt cheeks as hard as I could (which, from my position wasn't very hard). Mia made a noise like a horse and started to walk slowly.

I couldn't help it, my cock was soon rock hard as I walked Mia around the apartment, I made her walk from the living room to the dining room, round the table several times before taking her to the kitchen and back to the living room. I didn't need to use the riding crop but I did, I enjoyed hitting her with it and Mia didn't object. Well, with that gag in her mouth it's not like she could.

I sat on her back, slowly wanking myself as she moved. Eventually I couldn't take it anymore, I directed her back to the living room, making her walk to the armchair. I dismounted and pushed her against it, legs against the front of the chair, body pushed down into it. I took her arms and crossed them into the small of her back, then kicked her legs wide apart, exposing her cunt.

I dropped to my knees and lined my cock up against her cunt and pushed straight into her. A couple of weeks ago I'd speculated with Willow about what it would be like to fuck her tiny body and it was even better that I'd imagined, she was so tight. Mia moaned and pushed back against me and soon we were in synch, me thrusting as she pushed back against me. I still held the reins and pulled back on them, lifting her head up. I couldn't help it, I pulled harder than I should as I fucked her hard.

Mia was a good girl, she was grunting and groaning, showing her obvious pleasure at being fucked hard like an animal, she was panting and puffing as I used her. Every time I slapped her ass she moaned and squeezed her pussy tight against my cock. Christ, fucking Willow after this wasn't going to be the same.

I could feel my balls tightening, but I wasn't ready to cum yet. Instead I pulled out. Mia twisted her head to look at me, she looked disappointed that I'd stopped before I came. I smiled and rubbed my cock against her pussy, before lifting it and lining up with her asshole. I'd often wanted to use a girl's ass, but never found a girl that would let me. I looked at Mia, she knew what was coming next.

She unfolded her arms from her back and put them onto her ass cheeks and pulled them apart, inviting me to use her. Well, would you say no? I put the tip of my cock against her asshole, put my hands onto her hips and pulled her backwards as I thrust into her. Mia screamed in pain as I plunged in, getting three quarters of my cock in on that first thrust. Christ, and I thought her cunt was tight. I pulled back and thrust again and again, each time Mia cried out in pain as I fucked her ass. I could feel her squeezing her ass, clearly she'd been used like this before.

When she relaxed and accepted my full length I rutted her for all I was worth. I doubt she was getting anything out of the experience, other than pain in her ass and neck. My breathing was getting shallow and I started to pant.

"I'm going to cum slave . . . milk my cock Mia, squeeze me." Mia did as she was told, her already tight ass contracted even more as I fucked her harder. My balls tightened.

"I'm cumming, oh fuck Mia I'm cumming." I thrust one last time, sinking every inch of my cock into her ass. I let go of her hips and grabbed her tits instead, crushing them as I came, shooting load after load into her ass. After I'd finished cumming I stayed where I was, pinning her down with my weight. Eventually I pulled out and sat back and she cried out as I did so. I slapped Mia's ass as hard as I could.

"Fuck Mia, that was incredible." This may have been my first time fucking a girl's asshole, it sure as shit wasn't going to be my last. I stood up and pulled Mia's reins, moving her back into her kneeling position before sitting down in the chair. Mia smiled up at me as best she could. I felt sorry for her and reached behind her head to remove the gag. As soon as it came out she looked at me and spoke.

"Would you like me to clean you cock sir?" I nodded and Mia leaned in, taking my dirty member into her mouth. She sucked as hard as before, quickly cleaning my cock. She didn't stop until I pulled her off, then she moved back into her submissive pose. Despite her best efforts my erection had subsided. I needed a rest.

"Was that your first time using an asshole sir?"

I nodded. "How could you tell Mia?"

"Sir, if you're going to use a girl's ass you should take it slowly or use lube." I must have looked a bit upset as she spoke again quickly. "Sir, it doesn't matter about me, I'm a slave and must do as my master commands. But if you fuck Willow like that sir she'll scream and never let you do it again." I thought about what she said, I was grateful for the advice and thanked her.

"But what about you Mia? I've cum twice, I think it's time for you to cum."

"Thank you sir, but I'm not allowed to cum without my master's permission, and he's not here to grant permission sir."

Interesting.

"Get me a beer Mia."

"Yes sir." Mia crawled off and was back quickly. As much as I wanted to fuck her again I needed a break, so I got her back onto all fours, put my feet on her back and flicked the TV on. Jon would be back just after 11, so I had a couple more hours with her. We talked as I watched TV, she'd been interested in submission all her life, she just didn't know it. She lived for praise, pleasing and serving came naturally to her.

After a couple of beers I needed to pee, I almost stood up when I remembered Jon's words.

"I need to piss Mia." I wanted to see what she would do.

"Would you like me to drink your piss sir?" Yet again she surprised me, I thought I'd have to ask, I never thought she'd offer.

"Yes please Mia."

Mia got up off all fours and knelt in front of me, legs wide apart. She leaned in, took my cock into her hands and pulled it out, before leaning in and taking me into her mouth. Mia looked up at me and nodded, I took this to indicate that she was ready so I allowed a little piss to leak out of the end of my cock. Mia didn't back away or move, she just allowed her mouth to fill with piss. I was amazed that she managed to swallow without me having to take my cock out of her mouth, so what the hell? I just a stream of hot foul yellow liquid out of my cock, not pausing at all. Mia swallowed it all, never asking for me to stop, never refusing and not spilling a drop. What a girl. Jon was a lucky guy.

Twice more I used her mouth as a toilet until we headed towards 10pm. After the last piss when she pulled away I held her in place. Mia was intelligent, she started to suck, knowing that I wanted to use her again. I allowed her to suck me, when I was fully hard I pulled her off. Mia looked at me, she was waiting for instructions. While she waited she wanked me slowly.

I stood up and undid my trousers, letting them fall to the floor. I pushed forward, letting my ass hang off the edge of the seat. I put my hand on her head and pushed her down, opening my legs. Mia smiled at me, I couldn't believe that she could look so happy, surely she knew what I wanted?

Mia used her hands to push my legs further apart, she started with my balls and sucked them in turn, before licking down to my asshole. I gasped, this was another first for me. The sensation of having her tongue lick round my ass was incredible. Mia used her face to hold my cheeks apart, she continued to lick my asshole, she used her right hand to wank me as she licked, rimming me slowly. Mia slipped her left hand under me, I could feel her hand worming towards my ass, what did she plan?

I felt her suck her own finger for a moment, then it was against my asshole. I breathed heavily, I wasn't sure about this but, I was prepared to try. She was an expert in pleasing a man, I should let her do this.

Mia slowly pushed the tip of one of her fingers into my ass, only allowing a quarter of an inch in. She held it there for a few moments, I gasped to show I was OK with it before she pushed a little more in. Mia was fucking me with her finger, wanking me and licking my ass. Each time Mia would push a little more of her finger in until she was fucking me with her full finger. I could see what she'd meant, I must have really hurt her when I pushed my full length into her.

Mia didn't let up, she kept fucking, sucking and wanking until my cock started to twinge, Mia felt it and moved her head, taking me into her mouth just as I started to cum. I put my hands on her head and pushed down, shooting my cum straight into her throat.

"Fuck Mia, you're incredible."

When I released her she pulled her head off and smiled at me.

"Thank you sir, I'm glad you enjoy using me. Sir, I'm going to pull my finger out now, it will probably hurt you a little sir. Please discipline me if it hurts too much."

She was right, my ass tightened as she started to pull her finger out. I gasped a couple of times before it was fully out. I can't say I wanted to do this every time, but I was glad I'd tried. Mia looked at me, the raised her finger to her mouth and sucked it clean, before taking my softening cock back into her mouth.

I ran my finger through her hair, "Good girl," I said and Mia hugged my legs. I checked the clock, 30 minutes left. "One more thing to do." Mia took me out of her mouth and looked at me.

"Do you want to hurt me sir?"

I still couldn't believe that she could be so matter of fact about it. I nodded, then spoke.

"Mia, I . . . I don't want to hurt you, I, I just need to know that I can." My voice trailed off as I spoke.

"It's OK sir, my master gave you permission to hurt me as much as you want to. Please, do what you want." Mia was smiling bravely, but I could see that see wasn't looking forward to what was coming next.

"Mia, I'm not sure what to do. Can you advise me?"

Mia tried to be brave. "Well sir, you could just whip my ass with the riding crop, that's a standard punishment. My nipples are very sensitive, so I could get some clamps from Jon's room and you could put them on me and then pull them off? That hurts like hell sir. Master has a variety of whips, floggers and torture devices, would you like me to get a selection?" I nodded when she said this, I still wasn't sure about it but I had to try.

Mia crawled off, leaving me with the riding crop. I stood up and swished it through the air several times, imaging it hitting Mia's delicate rear and struck it against my thigh. Sure, I'd used it on her several times, but not hard. Next time was going to hurt. When Mia crawled back she put a selection of items on the floor in front of me. She then picked them up and ran through them. First she picked up a wide leather strap.

"This is the flogger sir, it is just about the most painful device to be flogged with, however, it doesn't leave much of a mark. The cane on the other hand hurts almost as much, but it's so thin that the marks last for days, sometimes weeks. This whip," she said, putting the wide leather flogger down and picking up a multi tailed whip, "doesn't hurt anywhere near as much, but still more than the riding crop." She put it down and picked up a candle. "My master sometimes likes to drip hot wax on my tits sir, then flog it off." Mia shuddered as she said that, clearly that wasn't something she was looking forward to. Next she picked up some device I didn't recognize. "This is a pair of nipple clamps sir. You can adjust the tightness here, making it more or less painful for me. I will take whatever setting you want to use." She said the last sentence very quietly.

"Also sir, I brought a lipstick. When you've finished with me can you write a score on my body for my master to see?" I nodded, accepting the nipple clamps she offered to me. I opened them and closed them, adjusting the tension on them. I picked what I thought was a middle setting and bent down. Mia stared at them, at the same time she bent her back and thrust out her tiny chest. I licked her nipples, enjoying the sensation of the metal bar in my mouth, teasing it behind my teeth. When I judged her nipples to be fully hard I opened the clamp and slid it behind the metal bars, before allowing it to close. Mia grimaced and gasped as they closed biting into her flesh.

"Does that hurt Mia?"

She looked at me like I was a moron, but she kept

her tone civil. "Yes sir, thank you for putting them on behind the bars. If they go on in front of my piercings that hurts more than you could believe." Christ, she was thanking me for hurting her. I'm pretty sure I'd be ripping them off and walking out. I guess that's why I'm not a slave and she is. I could feel my cock growing again, hurting her was turning me on.

I picked up the flogger, Mia asked if I wanted her to stand.

"No thank you Mia," I said, sitting down, "Please bend over my knee, ass out, legs on the floor." Mia did as she was ordered. I ran my right hand over her ass, then brought it up and slapped her hard. Mia took the first three blows in silence, before gasping as the fourth, fifth and sixth landed. I smiled, I could punish a girl, I knew that now. I checked the clock, 30 minutes to go.

I picked up the flogger and held it in front of Mia's face. She nodded and spoke.

"Would you like me to count sir?"

I thought for a moment. "That would be nice Mia," I replied.

I brought it up and then down onto her ass. I'm sure I could have done it faster standing, but this would do for now. Mia cried out as it bit into her skin, which was already turning red from me slapping her.

"One thank you sir," she managed to say, "Please may I have another?"

I didn't reply, I just felt my cock twinge again, I'd soon be fully hard. I brought up the flogger and then dropped it down onto her ass again, causing Mia to cry out again.

"Two thank you sir, please may I have another?" Mia's voice was weak, I was pretty sue she'd be crying soon.

Swish! "Three thank you sir, please may I have another?" Her voice was almost breaking, I could hear that she was holding back tears. Next time she'd break into tears.

Swish. I was right. The tears she was holding back came out and Mia started to sob. "Four thank you sir, please may I have another?"

Swish. The tears were flooding down her face and

it took her several seconds before she could speak. "Five thank you sir, please may I have another?" One more I decided. My cock was rock hard now, I wanted to use her ass again.

Swish. Mia screamed in pain through her tears. Eventually she managed to speak. "Six sir," she sobbed, "Please may I have another?"

"No Mia, that's enough." I pushed her off me and onto the floor, on her front. I kicked her legs apart and fell onto her, forcing my cock into her ass. Mia was still crying, she screamed in pain as I pushed deeper and deeper inside her ass.

"Thank you for punishing me sir," she managed to say through her tears, "Please fuck my ass sir, fuck it hard sir . . . hurt me with your cock sir . . . AAA-AAAARRRGGGHH . . . fuck that hurts sir . . . please don't stop sir . . . please . . . oh god this hurts sir." I was pounding away at her, my entire weight on her, pinning her down. Mia was still sobbing, in between her begging me to cum in her. I couldn't last for long, despite having already cum three times that night.

"I'm cumming, oh fuck I'm cumming," I yelled.

"Thank you sir, keep fucking me, yes," Mia sobbed

back as my balls contracted, pumping cum into her. When I'd finished I pulled out, Mia screamed again as my cock popped out, then I sat on the chair, looking down at her, her body was shaking, her ass red.

"Give me the whip," I told her. Mia moved and picked up the whip, she handed it to me before kneeling in front of me and then she started to suck my cock. I played with her, whipping her back but very gently as she cleaned me. I made her suck me until it was 10 before 11, my roommates would be back soon.

I pulled her off and looked at her. Her face was a mess, her makeup running where the tears (and my cum) had made it run. Her hair was fucked up from where I'd pulled and twisted it. Her nipples were a strange color from a lack of oxygen. I removed the clamps gently, as the blood seeped back in Mia cried out again.

"That hurts more than when they go on sir," she told me by way of an explanation.

I examined her back, it was red, but nowhere near as red as her ass. I smiled at Mia.

"I had a great night slave."

Mia's face broke into a smile. "I'm glad I pleased you sir. Please don't forget to mark me." I picked up the lipstick and wrote 10/10 on her chest. Mia didn't look down, I guess she didn't want to see the score. I told her to clean up and go to Jon's room to wait. I went to the door and took the chain off, then went to my room. I picked up my phone, shit Willow had sent me a dozen messages, idle chat at first, then asking me why I'd not replied. I told her I wasn't feeling well and had been in bed asleep, the same line Jon would have fed Paul and Steve. As soon as I hit send she started to reply, telling me to go back to bed and she'd see me tomorrow. I put the phone down and climbed into bed for real. I knew I could handle a slave girl now. Next was the real challenge, I had to enslave Willow. I fell asleep quickly, dreaming of fucking Willow and Mia at the same time.

WEDNESDAY
MARCH 25TH

I awoke with my alarm sounding at the usual time. Couldn't help myself, I woke with an erection and a head full of images from last night. My balls ached but fuck it, a quick wank settled me down. Then up and in the shower, then through into the kitchen. As usual, the coffee was in the percolator. Unusually Mia was there, wearing a skimpy silk robe. Shit I panicked when I saw her.

"Hi Jay," she said, pretending like last night hadn't happened, "Did you sleep well?"

"Er, yes thanks Mia," I managed to reply. I could feel my face turning red. "How did you sleep?"

"Not great, Jon locked me in a cage all night. He saw the marks on my body and figured you must have been disappointed with me, despite the 10/10 you awarded me." Mia was smiling as she said that.

"Look Mia, I'll speak to him, I wasn't disappointed at all."

"It's OK Jay, I'm his property. I usually spent one or two nights a week in there anyway. I like it, it reminds me that sharing his bed is a privilege, not a right." Mia picked up two cups of coffee and went back to Jon's room. I watched her leave, she was sexy as fuck, She must have known I was watching, outside Jon's room she put the coffee down and raised her robe, showing me her ass. Shit, it was bright red. Guilty barely begins to describe how I felt. I went back to my room to dress, soon after the four of us set off for work. I didn't get a chance to speak to Jon until later.

******

Just after 11 I was stood at the water cooler when I felt a slap on my back. I turned round, it was Jon.

"How was your night then buddy?" He asked me, "Worked out if you can control a slave?"

Suddenly I felt guilty as hell again, shit Mia was his girlfriend and he's loaned her to me. I'd not only taken advantage of her, but hurt her in the process. What the fuck would I feel like when I saw

Willow?

"Jon, it was fucking awesome, thank you so much. And I'm sorry if I went too far, I . . ." my voice faded out.

"Mate, I told you to do what you liked and it looks like you did. No, stop talking. I don't want to know. Not now, not ever. Understood?" I nodded. "Good."

"How can I ever repay you?

Jon thought for a moment. "Tell you what, if you manage to enslave Willow lend her to me for a night. Then we can call it even."

"If I enslave her it's a deal. One condition – I get to borrow Mia again."

"Sure we can swap. Or if you like I get them both for a night – we can alternate." We both laughed, this was so surreal, discussing women like they were property. Mia was, hopefully one day soon Willow would be as well. She'd messaged me several times to make sure I was OK, and she warned me she'd be round that night to make sure I was. Suddenly I felt guilty again. I went back to work.

******

I got back to the apartment just after six. Paul and Steve were still at work, dealing with some problem for a customer. Jon had left earlier. When I got in I dumped my bag and went to the kitchen for a beer. I opened the door and panicked again, at the kitchen table was Mia, she saw me and smiled.

"Hi Jay," she said. I looked down, shit, she was facing a mass of long red hair. Willow turned.

"Hi, how are you? Feeling better?"

I must have turned red, looking at the two girls. What had they been talking about? In my mind there could only be one thing. And it wasn't good news.

"I'm OK," I managed to stumble out.

"Sure?" said Willow, "You don't look good."

"I'm OK." She didn't look mad (in my albeit limited experience) redheads can be absolute lunatics if they feel that they have been wronged. Or you just don't understand them. Or a million other things. Still, she was in the kitchen and hadn't stabbed me, so it wasn't all bad.

Willow stood up and kissed me on the cheek. "I'll believe you then."

Mia stood up next, "I'll go back to Jon's room and leave you two alone. See you later."

When she left I looked at Willow. She was still smiling, Mia had clearly been as good as her word and not said a thing to her. I relaxed a little, the guilt hadn't left me though.

"Come on, let's stick the TV on for a bit," Willow said, taking my hand and walking me to the living room. Shit, it was just 24 hours ago I'd walked Mia through, though she'd been naked and dragged by her hair. My cock twinged again, thinking about it.

In the living room we watched the TV for half an hour or so until we were joined by Jon and Mia. We chatted then Jon suggested Olive Garden for our evening meal. It's only a couple of blocks away so we walked. I was quiet throughout the meal, Willow put it down to me not feeling great. I knew it was because anyone at that table could have exposed me for what I was.

We didn't go to a bar after, instead we went home. I stuck Netflix on and we went to bed. Later we fucked, I'll be honest, it didn't feel great. I was thinking about how much I'd enjoyed dominating Mia and a normal, Willow on her back fuck just didn't do it for me that night. What a shit I am.

FRIDAY MARCH 27TH

Friday night, time for the (now) regular game of poker.

"So," I said shuffling the cards and looking at Mia, "Last week we got to see you fully naked." Mia blushed – hell, I'd got to see a shit load more than that. "Same again, or do we take it further?"

"How much further can we go?" asked Abi. Stupid question. You can always go further.

"How about," asked Mia, "We play until two girls are naked?" Susie blushed and looked down, surely Steve had to lose at some point – I'd love to see her naked, only 18 years old with long blonde hair. Natural blonde too, according to Steve.

"Seems tame," I said, "how about we go a bit further."

The girls all looked at me.

"What are you thinking of Jay?" asked Mia. I was surprised that Willow hadn't asked that question.

"How about we play until two girls are naked, and then we all move to the living room, where they have to make out for five minutes." The girls started to look at each other as I spoke. Mia would do it, I think Abi would agree if Willow did, Susie would if the other two did so that Steve wouldn't have to miss out on the show. I continued to talk. I was enjoying coming out of my shell and leading the group a little, made a change from Steve deciding everything. I continued.

"And I mean proper making out, lots of tongues, kissing each other's breasts . . . ." I let my voice fade out as I finished the sentence. I looked directly at Mia. "Are you up for it Mia?" Mia looked at Jon who nodded. Mia then looked back at me.

"Sure," she said with a sly grin on her face. A pang of guilt came back to me as I looked at her, it didn't last for long. The fear of the events of Tuesday being revealed was starting to fade. Another week and I'd be over it.

I turned to Willow, smiled and winked at her. "You game?"

Willow stroked her hair then looked at Mia. The two girl's eyes met and they smiled at each other, Mia was encouraging Willow to say yes, she was mouthing the word YES to Willow.

"Sure Jay, I'm in."

"So am I," said Abi. That surprised me and Paul who turned to look at his girlfriend.

"And Susie will do it too, won't you?" added Smokes, not even looking at Susie. She just nodded silently. Rich bitch, she didn't think for one second she'd have to make good on Steve's promise. Rationally, I didn't think she'd have to either. Her time would come.

I picked up the cards and shuffled, Paul cut and I dealt the first hand.

******

We been playing for a few hours and we'd drunk several beers. I was trying hard not to get really drunk, I was alternating beers and a soft drink. I'd played quite well – Willow was in her bra, panties and shoes (she was turning into quite an exhibitionist). Abi was just in a matching set, Mia just her panties and of course Susie had only lost her shoes. One day . . . one day.

The current hand was interesting, we were all bidding, playing standard five card draw poker, so nothing on the table. I was holding three tens, not a great hand but it could win. The air in the room was full of cigarette smoke, one day they'd kill Steve (though knowing his luck he'd never be ill and it would be me that got lung cancer). The stakes were getting high, Paul had just gone all in. My turn, fold or all in. Shit.

"All in," I said, pushing my small pile of chips towards the center of the table. All eyes turned to Jon. He didn't speak, just pushed his stack of chips into the middle. All eyes were now on Smokes.

"All in boys," he said, pushing his pile of chips in. This was serious now, if he won three girls were about to lose an item of clothing. It was Paul to reveal his hand.

"Two pair, kings and queens."

"Fuck you," said Jon, throwing his cards in, "Mia,

lose the panties."

By rights I should have showed my hand but I paused, watching as Mia removed her tiny panties and stood there, just like last week, as naked as the day she was born. We all studied her body for a few moments, ah it brought back many happy memories for me. When I realized I was staring I stopped and looked round the table, expecting to see everyone staring at me, but it was OK, they were all looking at Mia. Jon broke the silence.

"Come on Jay, let's see your hand."

I put them down on the table and showed my hand of three tens. Would it win?

Would it fuck. With agonizing slowness Smokes put his cards down and fanned them out. eight, seven, six, five, four. Bastard. We looked at Paul, then at Abi. She smiled and reached behind her back, unhooking her bra slowly and removing it, hanging it on the back of Paul's chair before folding her hands behind her back again. She smiled at us, her tits were rock solid and her light brown skin was such a contrast to Susie, Mia and Willow. Now it was Willow's turn. I didn't need to speak to her, I just turned to watch as she pushed her hair behind her back and slowly, ever so slowly removed her bra, holding an arm over her nipple line, swirling the lacy bra round a finger before throwing it over the table to Smokes. Finally she pulled her arm back to reveal her nipples, then folded her arms behind her back.

Eventually we turned back to the game, shit she was enjoying showing off.

"OK boys, Mia's naked now. Do I get to keep playing?"

"Sure," said Smokes, blowing out more smoke, "But she has to perform a forfeit if you lose again."

"What kind of forfeit?"

"Don't know yet, I'll think of something." Jon smiled, letting us know that Mia would perform the forfeit, whatever it was. I handed out another $5,000 in chips for the three losers and we settled down to play. As Paul dealt I spoke to Willow.

"Open a window please Willow, let some air in and blow some smoke out." I turned to look at her, the dining room has huge widows looking out onto the street and the apartments beyond. If anyone was watching, they'd see her almost naked body.

Willow looked at me, would she do it? After a few seconds she nodded and turned and walked to the windows. Willow pulled back the drapes and opened one, two and then the third window a couple of inches. Instantly I could feel the fresh air coming in and the smoke dissipating a little. Willow stepped back and closed the drapes, then walked back to behind me. Her nipples stood out like little bullets, rock hard from their exposure to the night air.

Paul had dealt two hole cards each, the game was Texas hold'em. We all passed on the first round. Paul burnt the top card and dealt three more face up. I had shit all, if anyone bet I'd fold and just lose the $500 blind I'd paid in. Jon passed as did Smokes, Paul paid in $1,000.

"Fold," I said, throwing my cards back to Paul as dealer.

"4,000, all in," said Jon.

"All in," said Smokes, pushing his chips in. Why not I guess, he was $40,000 or more ahead. There was no way Susie was losing any clothes this round.

"Fuck it," said Paul and pushed in his remaining chips. Willow was safe, at least for this round. Paul burnt the top card and dealt one more, there was a pair of eights on the table now with a four and five. Paul shrugged and burnt the next card, then flipped the river card, nine of clubs. Interesting, three clubs on the table and the making of a straight. I was glad I'd dropped out, my Jack and two wouldn't have won this round.

You could have cut the tension with a knife. I'd watched lesbian porn, fuck who hasn't, but watching real live naked girls making out six feet away from me? Shit, I really hoped I wouldn't cum in my pants just from watching. It was Jon's turn to show first.

"Dead man's hand," he said, shrugging. Aces and eights, not a bad hand by any stretch. "Hopefully I make it through the night," he added smiling.

"Nice," said Smokes, "Never actually seen that in a game before." He took a drag on his Camel before revealing his cards. "But not as nice as a Queen high flush in clubs."

"Oh for fuck's sake," said Paul, clearly annoyed and throwing his cards into the middle of the table. The game was over. Abi looked around the table, she was shaking a little. Nervously she put her hands onto her lacy white panties.

"Stop," said Smokes. Abi didn't need to be told twice. She took her hands out of her panties and looked back at Smokes. "I've got an idea .... Come with me." Steve stubbed out his camel and stood up. Like docile children we all stood up and followed our leader to the living room. One bonus of changing rooms like that, Steve doesn't smoke in that room.

"Back in five," he said heading off to his room. I sat on one of the chairs, Willow sat on my lap, my face level with her nipples. Jon winked at me and sat in one of the others, he directed Mia to kneel on the floor in front of him, facing outwards. She did as told, initially knees together until Jon ordered her to open wide.

"I lost Mia, show them what you've got."

I couldn't take my eyes off her pussy, shit four days ago I'd been fucking that sweet, tight hole. I looked at Willow, she was staring at Mia as well A quick glance at the couch were Paul, Abi and Susie were sitting showed that they were all looking at Mia, kneeling at her master's feet in total submission.

"Give me a hand please," said Steve from the corridor. Paul pushed Abi and she stood up, wearing nothing but her panties and she walked to the door and went out. She was back seconds later, pulling a mattress. Steve and Abi dumped it on the floor, the couch and chairs formed a U shape, the table that usually lived in the middle of the U had been pushed to one side and the mattress took it's place. For all his faults Steve is loaded, he's spent a couple of hundred bucks on a new mattress just to watch two girls kiss. What a guy.

He sat down and pulled Susie onto his knee. "Stand on the mattress Abi, arms behind your back." Abi stood up and obeyed the order. "OK Mia, here's your forfeit," continued Steve, "Go to Abi, crawl, don't walk, then remove her panties, very slowly." Mia looked at Jon who nodded, Abi watched then looked at Paul, pleading with her eyes to save her from this humiliation. Paul just shook his head and then Abi nodded, resigned to her fate.

Mia crawled slowly to Abi, she circled the mattress twice, giving us all a long look at her. Fuck, her ass was a little red still, my fault. In my pants I could feel my cock starting to grow. Mia could work a crowd. After her second time round Mia crawled onto the mattress and knelt up in front of Abi, her mouth level with Abi's public mound. Mia smiled at Abi, then raised her hands, putting them on Abi's knees and sliding them up Abi's long, dark legs. Abi formed her fists into balls and closed her eyes when Mia slipped her fingers inside Abi's panties.

"Stop," said Jon, we all looked at him, was he going to call a halt to this? He'd better not. "Mia, fold your arms behind your back." He lowered his voice and spoke very softly. "Mia, use your teeth to take them off."

"Sexy," whispered Willow. She was right, how much sexier could this get?

Mia was a good girl, she did as she was told. She raised herself slowly, raising her ass up. Mia leaned in and opened her mouth, pushing her jaw backwards so her upper teeth stuck out a little, she pushed her face against Abi's stomach and took the material into her mouth, then pulled down. She moved the panties a little, then moved to Abi's hip and repeated the move. Willow put her hand on my cock, I was rock hard now and we exchanged a glance as she felt it.

Mia moved round Abi, each time lowering her panties a half inch. I saw Steve adjust himself, he was clearly enjoying the show. Even stuck up

Susie couldn't take her eyes away. When Mia got the panties over her hips she pulled them down in one swift move and they fell to the floor. I was pleased to see that Abi's pussy had a little tuft of hair as a landing strip. Abi's fists were tensing and relaxing, she was psyching herself up for what was about to come. In front of her Mia resumed her submissive kneeling pose.

Abi didn't move until Paul told her he kneel down and face Mia. "Get your knees touching," he ordered her as she had her knees together. Abi was shaking as she slowly opened her legs wide, revealing her pussy to the audience.

"OK girls," I said, "Showtime, and remember you'll be making out until I decide you've completed five minutes." Abi raised her arms and put her hands over her own breasts to cover them. Mia was going to have to take the lead. And she did, she raised her ass up (she is much shorter than Abi) and put her hands onto Abi's head, running her fingers through Abi's long black hair. Abi finally opened her eyes and looked into Mia's. Then Mia leaned in, she paused when their lips were an inch apart before pulling Abi's head towards her. Their lips touched briefly before Mia released Abi.

They looked at each other for a moment before Mia leaned in again to kiss Abi. This time Abi extended a hand, I think she meant to push Mia away but somehow she ended up cupping Mia's naked breast. Mia paused and looked down, Abi didn't take her hand away and Mia put one of her hands on top of it, holding it in place. Mia looked back at Abi who's mouth moved (briefly) into a smile. They kissed again, this time their mouths opened and for the first time Abi kissed another girl (Abi confirmed this later, I'm pretty sure it wasn't Mia's first time with another woman).

I watched, we all watched as Mia and Abi kissed, their tongue entwined, saliva connecting their mouths when they separated. Mia massaged Abi's hand on her breast until Abi started to play with it herself, when she started Mia put her hands onto Abi's firm athletic chest. Abi's nipples were soon rock hard, I was mentally begging Mia to suck on them but she stuck to the script and they just kissed, caressing each other's breasts but not licking or sucking. Abi took the lead next, she kissed Mia's neck and then sucked on her ears. I was desperate to touch myself (or have Willow do it) but I'd have to wait.

I looked round the room, Willow, Steve, shit everyone was glued to watching the lesbian scene in front of us – even Susie was gripped, she had her arms wrapped round Steve, she wasn't even blinking. I checked my watch, they'd been making out for almost 10 minutes. Fuck it, another five minutes wouldn't hurt anyone, and besides, they didn't look like they were in any hurry to stop any time soon.

All good thing come to an end and eventually Abi looked at me. She didn't speak but the inference was clear. "OK girls, you can stop. That's five minutes easy." Mia didn't release Abi straight away, instead she pulled her back and they kissed softly, just on the lips a couple of times.

Smokes pushed Susie off his knee, "If you'll excuse us folks . . ." and he took Susie's hand and led her out of the room. Willow and I were next, with Jon and Mia just behind. As soon as we were in my room I closed the door, when I turned round Willow was pulling off her panties. She was on the bed, on her back.

"Fuck me Jay, just fuck me now." Well, would you say no? I undid my belt and pulled at my 501s, I love button flies, they just ripped open and I pulled them down, got my underpants down at the same time. I didn't bother with my shirt and left my pants around my ankles. I hopped across the room and fell onto the bed, lying on top of Willow. She pushed her tits upwards and I pushed my cock into her sopping wet cunt.

"Oh God yes," cried Willow as I entered her, "Jesus you feel big tonight." My cock had never been so hard as I started to fuck her. "That's it, fuck me Jay, really fuck me, hard. Faster, come on Jay, fuck me hard . . . yes, that's it." Then something new from her. "Choke me Jay . . . choke me . . . put your hand on my throat and choke me." I did as she asked and wrapped my hand on her throat and squeezed.

"Come on Jay . . . I can still talk . . . squeeze my fucking throat, I don't want to breathe." I waited until she took a deep breath then I tightened my hand on her throat. Willow opened her eyes wide, she was trying to breathe out but my grip on her throat held and she couldn't do it. I was really hammering her now, her head started to go red as I held my grip. Willow put a hand onto my wrist and tried to pull my hand away, not very hard but I just ignored her and kept fucking my girl.

I'd held her throat for about a minute when her body started to convulse, she was cumming, I could feeling her bending under me, she was scratching at my back and trying to pull my hand away. Her orgasm set me off and I started to cum, I found it very exciting to control her like that.

"I'm cumming Willow, holy fuck I'm cumming." As soon as I started to cum I released the grip on her neck and Willow breathed out and in rapidly.

"I'm . . . still . . . cumming Jay, oh . . . fuck I'm . . . still . . . cumming. Don't stop, . . . don't you . . . fucking . . . stop . . . Oh Shit I'm going to . . . cum again . . . YESSSS"

She was breathing deeply but was starting to slow down as the oxygen in her blood stream was replenished. Eventually she pushed me off and rolled onto her side to look at me.

"That was so intense! I love you Jay," she said.

I kissed her head and said the same. We snuggled up and went to sleep.

SATURDAY
MARCH 28TH

When I awoke Willow was looking at me, the duvet was down far enough to reveal the top of her breasts, nipples still hidden. I looked at her, holy fuck her neck was red from where I'd choked her the night before.

"Willow, I . . . I," words failed me as I looked at her neck.

"I hope you weren't about to apologize for any-thing," she said, "If I get to cum like that you're damn well going to choke me again. It was fucking incredible Jay, I was still cumming from my first orgasm when I came again."

She hugged me, phew. I thought she'd been about to terminate our relationship, and I didn't want that.

"Jay, yesterday, did you enjoy watching Abi and Mia making out?"

I nodded, stupid question. Who would want to watch a pair of hot, naked girls making out five feet away from you? The only thing that could have made it better was if they'd carried on and gone the whole way. Or asked me to join them. Actually, there are many ways it could have been better.

"Did you look at Mia? Her ass? It was red, looks like she'd been spanked." I couldn't help it, I could feel my face going as red as Mia's ass. Thank fuck the only light in the room was crawling round the edge of the drapes, Willow wouldn't be able to see.

"Have you ever spanked a girl Jay?"

"No," I lied, going even redder.

"Would you like to? Would you like to spank me?"

Oh God yes, I'd love to spank you Willow, spank you as hard as I'd spanked Mia four days ago. Did I say this? Did I fuck. Instead I took the cowards way out.

"Depends, would you like to be spanked?" It was out in the open.

Willow slipped her hand across and took my cock into it. She started to wank me slowly.

"Yes Jay," she whispered, "I've been a bad girl and I should be spanked for it Jay." Her voice was soft a sultry, teasing me. My cock was growing rapidly. "Tell me I've been a bad girl Jay, I've had dirty thoughts and should be punished for it Jay, tell me how bad I am."

"You have been bad haven't you Willow?" I replied. She nodded and I carried on. "Watching lesbians kissing, you should have been disgusted shouldn't you?" Willow was raised in a strict Catholic family, I'd met her parents and could guess at how she'd been raised.

"That's right Jay," she replied, "I watched a sin being committed and it turned me on. I'm such a bad girl Jay, what will you do with me?"

I sat up, Willow didn't release my cock, instead she put her head on my lap and took me into her mouth. She twisted round, getting onto all fours, pushing her ass towards my right hand. Fuck it. I raised my hand up and swatted her ass, not hard, I didn't want her to back off instantly. She took her head away from my cock.

"Is that all you've got Jay, or should I get a real man to punish me?" She took me back into her mouth. Right, you fucking asked for this. Literally. I raised my hand up and this time hit her peach posterior much harder. Willow made a sound, but didn't stop sucking my cock. I felt her jaw move, fuck it was exciting, knowing that she was having to control herself when no doubt she wanted to clench her jaws together. She hadn't asked me to stop so I hit her again and again, each time she'd make a noise but she never stopped sucking my cock.

Willow put a hand between her legs and started to masturbate, judging by the speed it was moving at it wouldn't be long before she came.

Whack! Willow made a high pitched noise in her throat. I started to move my hips, holding the back of her head with my spare hand and fucking her mouth. She wasn't as good at oral as Mia, but she was learning quickly. Every time I struck her she shuddered and moved and I knew she's cum soon.

I started to speak to her as I used her mouth and

spanked her ass. "You're a bad girl Willow, watching lesbians like that, you should be punished." Whack! "Bad girls get punished, you know that now." Whack! "I'll keep punishing you until I think you've had enough." Whack! Her body was trembling she was going to cum soon. "And don't you fucking cum until I do bitch." Whack!

On about my 30th blow my balls tightened. "I'm cumming Willow, oh yes . . . yes . . . YESSSS." I hit her particularly hard on the last strike as I started to pump cum into her willing mouth, as soon as she tasted my cum her hips bucked and her legs gave way, she was cumming hard. Willow held me there, when I finished cumming she sucked gently before taking me out and swallowing my load.

"Thank you for letting me cum Jay, that was so intense, having to hold it. I've never been controlled like that before."

I kissed her and offered my hand to her face. "Kiss the hand that punished you Willow." She kissed my hand, then licked it before sucking my fingers.

"Promise me you'll spank me again sometime, it was so hot."

"I'll spank you again," I winked and smiled as I spoke, "Next time you deserve it."

Willow and I laughed. I was in the mood now, I raised my hand and slapped her again. Willow looked at me, why had I done that?

"Now be a good girl and go get us some coffee."

"Yes sir," she replied and got out of bed. At the door she paused and looked at me, I picked up my phone and ignored her. Willow opened the door and went out, still naked. She was back a couple of minutes later. Willow climbed into bed and offered me a cup. I took it from her and sipped it.

"Jay," she said, sipping the boiling hot liquid, "There's something I've been meaning to ask."

"Sure, what is it?"

"We've been dating for what, 18 months? Every morning I wake up here there's a pot of fresh coffee been made. It's not on a timer plug and the machine isn't even out when we go to bed. Who makes it?"

Mia, I almost replied. Instead I came out with, "Good question. I think Jon once told me Mia is a very light sleeper and she wakes up much earlier than anyone else, she likes a cup when she gets up and so she makes a pot."

Willow blew across the top of her cup. "Mmmmm." She was clearly thinking about it. As I said it I thought it sounded unbelievable. It was close to the truth. At least Willow hadn't asked me who did the cleaning, then I'd have been on a very difficult slope.

We sat in silence and drank our coffee.

******

Willow had to study during the day (as did the other girls), exams were only 6 weeks away so the boys and I left them alone in the apartment and we went out. It was unseasonably warm so we went to a park and played touch football for most of the morning, then went to one of our favorite restaurants for lunch. Smokes had left $50 out on the kitchen table so the girls could phone out for food, he was very generous like that.

The afternoon passed slowly for us, we went down to the seafront and walked and talked, planning out the next poker evening. We'd have to warn the girls, as usual Mia wouldn't have an issue with it, I was pretty sure Willow would go along, Paul said Abi would, if Mia and Willow would and Smokes assured us that Susie would, mainly as he was going to win.

"How was your night with Abi," I asked Paul, "Was she OK with you, I mean, she didn't look that happy at having to kiss Mia."

Paul thought for a moment, "Abi was OK, I think. In the end watching her I thought she looked like she enjoyed it. She just had to overcome her natural inhibitions." Paul laughed, "And when I got her back to my room she was like a wild animal when we fucked. Awesome." We all laughed. "How about Willow?"

I don't like talking about what goes on in our bedroom, but I figured I didn't really have a choice after Paul had opened up like that.

"She was pretty turned on by watching Abi and Mia, more than she'd care to admit." I smiled, "Yes, I had a wild night as well."

"My night sucked," offered Steve. "Susie wouldn't stop talking about how disgusting it was, and how we were all perverts to (a) make them do it and (b) watch like we did." He took a long toke on his Camel.

"As far as I could see she watched pretty carefully," Jon said, "And then she talks about it all night. Mate, she's just in denial about her own repressed lesbian urges." We all laughed at that. Later we went to a bar, before returning to the apartment just after six. The girls had all finished studying for the day and we went out as a group for the night, eating something and then hitting a few bars. This really is a great life for a young man, free rent in a superb apartment, high income and pretty much entirely disposable.

******

We got back just after one am, all pretty drunk and we went to our rooms. Willow and I kissed and I removed her top and bra, revealing her creamy white breasts. I never tire of this, redheads have such pale skin. After a few minutes I needed to use the bathroom so I excused myself for a couple of minutes.

When I came back Willow had removed all her clothes and was on her knees, legs wide apart, just like Mia and Abi the night before. I looked at her, fuck she was sexy. Between her legs was the cord from my dressing gown. My cock pulsed, she wanted me to tie her up. We'd never tried bondage before.

"Bind my arms behind my back please sir," she said, "Then do whatever you want with me sir, I won't say no."

I walked round her, Willow didn't move, she kept her head and body absolutely still, hands palms upwards on her thighs. The only sign of life from her was her breasts, rising and falling as she breathed in and out. I couldn't resist her.

I walked in front of Willow and picked up the cord. She looked up at me and raised her right arm. I tied the cord round her wrist, then stepped behind her and knelt down. I pulled her arm behind her, she moved the left one behind her as well, then I tied her wrists together. There was a lot of the cord left, so I pulled it up and tied it to her left elbow, then dragged the remainder to her right elbow and pulled her elbows together. I got them to about four inches apart when Willow made a noise.

"Does that hurt Willow?"

"Yes sir," she replied.

"Not complaining are you?"

"No sir."

I paused then I leaned in and whispered into her ear, "Ask me to pull your elbows closer together Willow."

I couldn't see her face but I knew she was smiling. "Please sir, pull my elbows closer together. Make it hurt please sir."

I did as she asked, tightening the cord until her elbows were only two inches apart, then I wrapped the cord round her elbows so that the rope wouldn't bite too deeply into her flesh. When there was a little left I tied it off, then stood up and walked in front of Willow. She looked up at me.

"Does this hurt you Willow?" I asked.

"Yes sir, it hurts my shoulders." I looked at her, her breasts had raised up slightly from having her arms tied behind her back. She looked hotter than ever. I remembered something, in a drawer I had a blindfold, a relic from a holiday to France.

"Close your eyes Willow and keep them closed until I say you can open them."

She smiled again, "Yes sir," she said in a low, sexy voice. Willow closed her eyes, fuck she looked hot, arms bound, her long red hair cascading over her shoulders, half down her front and half down her back. I had to tear my eyes away from her as I looked in my drawer. After a few minutes I found it and returned to her. I slipped it over her head and covered her eyes – this wasn't a free one from a flight, but one I'd paid real dollars for, it was excellent.

"Can you see anything?"

"No sir," she replied, "Just a faint outline of light round the edge of the blindfold sir."

It was time. I removed my clothes and let them fall to the floor. I took the belt from my pants and placed it in my hand, folding it in two so that I could lash her with it. I was very careful to do this silently, when I lashed her the first time I wanted it to come as a complete surprise. I wouldn't hit her anywhere as hard as I'd hit Mia. Well, not this first time in her submission anyway.

My cock was rock hard, it was time to use Willow's mouth. I moved to between her legs, the end of my cock was two or three inches away from her mouth and about level with her eyes. I wanted her to work out what to do, I didn't want to force my cock into her mouth. Not yet anyway.

I stayed still for 20, 30 seconds before Willow worked it out. She raised herself up and little so her mouth was just about level with my cock, then she leaned forward until her lips touched the tip of my penis. She stayed like that for a moment, I could feel the breath from her nose on my helmet, shit that was hot. She opened her mouth and pushed out her tongue, licking the end of my cock. I think if I'd been sober I'd have cum there and then.

Willow opened wide and took me into her mouth. She closed her lips on my cock and sucked, pulling me into her willing mouth, so hot and wet in there. Willow sucked hard, inch after inch of my cock disappeared until only a couple of inches were outside her mouth. Willow then opened wider and pushed out her tongue, licking the base of my cock, flicking the top of my ball sack.

I groaned in delight, Willow was getting better at this by the day. Another couple of weeks and I think she'd be as good, or even better than Mia. Willow started to suck up and down, taking me deeper with each suck until she gagged, she pulled back, my cock leaving her mouth as she coughed and spluttered. Fuck it, I lifted my belt up and brought it down into her left breast. Hard enough that she would feel it, not so hard that she'd scream in pain.

"Ow," she said. I'd never struck her before, but after my experience with Mia I knew that I enjoyed doing it to a woman. What kind of sick fuck am I?

"Don't take my cock out of your mouth unless I pull you off slut," I said to her in a menacing voice.

"Yes sir, I'm sorry I did sir. It won't happen again sir."

Willow straightened up and took me back into her mouth and started to suck again. She wasn't taking me as deep this time round, clearly she didn't want to choke and have to pull away. Tough shit girl, I wanted her to gag. It's not just the sensation of being that deep in her mouth that I enjoyed, it was the power and control over making her gag that I loved.

I put my hand onto the back of her head and pulled her down until Willow gagged again. Poor Willow, she started to splutter and cough, she tried to pull back but I wouldn't let her, instead I just pulled her tighter to me. Her back through was

stronger than my arm and she succeeded in escaping, I allowed her to cough and splutter for a
while. Eventually Willow managed to speak.

"I'm sorry sir," she said, reaching for my cock. I
slapped her face, knocking her head sideways. I
bent down and put the belt round her neck, forming a loose collar and leash. I pulled on it, dragging
Willow forwards. She bent forward, under normal circumstances I expect she would have put
her arms forwards to take her weight, but she of
course couldn't manage this. Instead she started
to shuffle on her knees, making slow progress.

I walked Willow slowly to the door and turned
her round, so she had her back to the door. Now
she had now where to go when I fucked her throat.
Willow knew what was coming, she opened her
mouth and I pushed my cock inside her willing
mouth. I took a tight grip on the makeshift leash,
I could use this to control her breathing and put
my hands on her head. I started to fuck her throat.
When she struggled or gagged I didn't let up. Willow tried to pull away but the door held her firm,
when she twisted to the side I used my hands to
move her back.

This was incredible, the best blowjob of my life.
Except it wasn't a blowjob – a blowjob is given
by the girl, I was fucking her mouth and throat,

using it like a cunt. In and out, in and out I used her mouth without regard for her. It didn't take long until my balls started to tighten and pulse, I pulled out of Willow's mouth and wanked myself, Willow coughed and spluttered as I shot my load over her face, her hair and some into her mouth.

"Fucking hell Willow, that was incredible."

When she stopped coughing she spoke quietly. "I'm glad you enjoyed yourself sir."

I took pity on her and removed the blindfold, the light level was low but she still blinked as she adjusted to the light. I bent down and tucked the belt into it's loop, forming the belt into a collar, then helped her to stand.

"Sir, may I please use the bathroom?"

I looked at her and smiled. "Sure."

I turned her round and reached for the cord.

"Sir, please don't untie me." I turned her back and looked at her.

"Sure you want to do this?" Willow nodded, so I opened the door and she went through it, face covered in cum, collar on her neck, arms bound behind her back. I got into bed and waited for her to return.

Willow came in and used her body to close the door, then got into the bed beside me. She snuggled up and looked at me.

"Are you going to leave me tied all night sir?"

The way she asked my indicated that she expected me to say yes, so I just nodded.

"Sleep well sir," Willow said. I kissed her and called her a kinky bitch, she just laughed. "Sir, I'm learning what you like. And what I like." I turned the light out and we went to sleep. Well, I went to sleep, I doubt Willow would get much bound like that.

SUNDAY
MARCH 29TH

I awoke late, I checked the clock, it was almost 10am. Beer and a throat fuck from a willing submissive, what better way to spend a night? I turned over, Willow wasn't lying next to me, I sat up. She was on the floor, kneeling, legs together. I looked at her.

"Good morning slave." There, I'd said it. I'd called her slave. Willow raised her head and looked at me, then opened her legs wide to show me her pussy. She still had the makeshift collar on her neck, there was a red stripe on her left breast from where I'd whipped her with my belt. Her arms were still bound tightly behind her back. She spoke to me, softly.

"Good morning sir, how did you sleep?" Was she playing or taking this seriously? I'd find out later.

"I slept very well Willow. How about you?"

"I barely slept at all sir, this isn't very comfortable."

"Would you like me to free you?"

"It's not my choice sir, is it?"

No, I conceded, no it isn't. I smiled, I was enjoying my power over her. I looked at her ravishing body, I wanted to fuck her. And looking at her, Willow wanted to be fucked as well. She been a great mouth-cunt last night, it was time to repay the favor.

"Get up on the bed, on your back."

Willow stood up as gracefully as she could (hell, I was just impressed that she could stand without falling). She climbed up onto the bed and struggled to the middle before she lay on her back, her head at the top of the bed. I put a pillow under her head and then got off. I found the blindfold and slipped it over her head, rendering her unable to see.

Mia had left me a couple of ropes, I picked them up and tied one round her left ankle and the other round her right. I think she knew what was coming as she opened her legs wide. I smiled, she was becoming so submissive in bed. I took the other ends and pulled them tight before securing them to the bedframe, leaving her pussy totally exposed and ready for me.

One final touch, I opened a drawer and pulled out a second belt. I folded it in half, I wasn't going to punish Willow anywhere near as hard as I had done last night, but I wanted to mix pain and pleasure in her psyche.

I paused before starting to look at her gorgeous body. Her huge breasts had hardly moved, her smooth, hairless pussy was on display. She was moving and writhing on the bed, she was clearly very excited at what was about to come.

I climbed onto the bed between her legs, I put the belt down quietly so she couldn't hear it. I put my hands on her knees and started to kiss her legs. I started on her thighs and kissed/licked my way down to her feet. Willow has very sensitive feet, she hates them being tickled but she'd happily have me caress them for hours.

I ran my tongue over her feet, before sucking each toe in turn. Willow was making quiet moaning sounds, she was clearly enjoying the attention. Eventually I moved over to her other foot and started to suck her other foot, before working my way back up her leg.

Willow clearly expected me to suck her pussy, I could see it glistening in the dull light, instead I ignored it and pushed my tongue into her belly button. Her whole body moved when I did this, she loves having her belly button licked. I put my hands up onto her shoulders and pulled myself up, I paused as my cock lined up with her hole before thrusting in. Willow's mouth opened wide and she gasped, she loves that first sensation when I penetrate her.

I didn't fuck her then, I just lay still, buried inside her. I put my elbows onto the bed to support my weight and started to kiss and lick her breasts, ignoring her nipples for the moment. I circled them with my tongue before eventually sucking her nipples, as soon as my tongue touched them they became rock hard. Willow's mouth was open, she was panting. Under me she started to buck her hips, I was still but my cock was sliding in and out of her, she was fucking me.

"Lie still slave," I whispered in her ear.

"Fuck," she gasped before stopping moving, "I mean yes sir."

"Good girl," I said to her.

This was hard for her I could see. But this was about her surrendering control and me controlling her. It was clearly a struggle for Willow to be still but she managed it. Almost. She was wriggling her feet.

I kissed my way back to her pussy and picked up the belt. I paused, my face an inch from her sweet cunt. Willow couldn't help herself, she pushed her body down the bed. Time to teach her who was in control. As quietly as I could I lifted the belt and brought it down onto her breasts – not so hard as to kill the moment, but hard enough that she'd feel some pain.

"Ow, fuck," she gasped.

"Lie still Willow."

"I'm trying sir . . . I'm trying . . . OW." I hit her second time, then a third and fourth before I realized she couldn't keep still. Poor Willow. I moved a little and licked her from her asshole all the way up along her labia. As soon as my tongue touched her she started to writhe, unable to control herself any longer so I had no choice, I lashed her again with the belt.

I fucked her with my tongue as I continued to whip her tits, I wasn't going to stop until she came. Willow was gasping and panting, begging for release in between yelling in pain as I periodically whipped her tits with the belt.

"I'm cumming Jay . . . oh fuck Jay I'm cumming . . . don't stop . . . please Jay, don't . . ."

Willow's lifted her body off the bed, sitting upright as she came. I could feel her trying to bring her legs together but the restraints held her tight in place. When she lay back down I threw the belt away and lifted myself on top again and fucked her hard. It was only seconds before I started to cum, pumping in and out of her.

As we lay there we kissed, then Willow spoke to me.

"That was incredible sir," she said, "You got everything just right."

"Did you enjoy being tit whipped?"

Willow blushed, "Yes sir. Promise me you'll do it again some time?"

"Oh, I will Willow, I will."

Eventually as my cock shrank I rolled off her and untied Willow. I looked at her tits, they were bright red from where I'd been lashing them. I felt a bit guilty, even if she'd enjoyed it. I ordered her to lie on her front as I undid the arm restraints. Her shoulders were stiff and it took Willow a few moments to be able to move again. When she could she got off the bed and knelt back on the floor. I sat on the bed in front of her and she took my soft cock into her mouth.

"You like the taste of pussy, don't you."

Willow made a soft noise of agreement.

"And you like being submissive don't you."

Stronger noise of agreement.

"What did you enjoy most about this morning Willow?"

She stopped sucking and pulled off my cock.

"When you called me 'Good Girl' sir, that was degrading, humiliating and, and, and I loved it sir."

I let Willow suck me for another five minutes or so before I pulled her off. I wasn't going to cum again straight away. She looked up at me, worried, clearly thinking she'd done something wrong.

"How about getting us coffee?"

"My pleasure sir." Willow stood up, she still had the makeshift belt collar on her neck and looked every inch the submissive slave. "Sir, do you want me to go naked?"

I smiled. "Sure." Willow didn't argue, she opened the door and left the room. I went for a piss, when I came back she was on her knees, the coffee on the small bedside table.

"Did you see anyone?" I asked.

Willow blushed, "Mia caught a glimpse of me sir."

Interesting. We drank our coffee, then I removed the belt from her neck and we went for a shower. As soon as I removed her collar she stopped calling me sir. I preferred it when she called me sir, I'd have to do this again.

*****

Willow and I met Jon, Paul, Paul, Abi and Mia in the living room later on, Steve and Susie came through a few minutes later. We went out for brunch then the girls all left to go back to their apartments so they could study. We wouldn't be seeing them again until Monday at the earliest. There was a new Thai restaurant that we wanted to try in the evening, over the meal we talked about the Friday night poker games.

"Thing is," said Smokes, "how do we go one better than last week?"

"Well," said Paul, "I can think of one way." We all looked at him. "Take it to the next level. Don't stop at kissing and fondling. Losing two girls have to fuck while the rest of us watch."

I picked up my beer and drank a bit. This works for me.

"Questions is," said Jon, breaking the silence as we all thought about it, "would they go for it? I mean, Mia will, naturally. But how about Susie, Willow or Abi? Would any of them do it?"

"We have to ask them," said Smokes, "And then more than that I think, we have to get them to sign a contract saying that they will."

"How about," I added, "If we spice it up as well."
They all looked at me – spice it up beyond live lesbian sex in the living room? "Winner of the round gets to remove the losing girl's item of clothing? We all enjoyed watching Mia remove Abi's panties, so how sharing the fun?"

We all thought about it. "Let's take them out on Tuesday and discuss it," said Smokes, "That means we can discuss it in private with each of them on Monday."

That would work.

MONDAY
MARCH 30TH

I looked across the table at Willow, she managed to make eating with chop sticks look sexy. Me? I'm a shoveller, I've probably eaten two thirds of the Chinese banquet.

"So," said Willow, chasing a piece of chicken round her bowl, "What's the plan for Friday? How are you going to top last week?"

Well, I hadn't expected her to open the conversation. I was working my way up to it, figuring that this was an after dinner conversation, five beers into the evening type of discussion. I picked up my beer and drank some, searching for the courage to discuss what we had planned.

"The thing is Willow," I said, "We want to go one better than last week."

"I bet. And how do you plan to top it? Or should I say, how do you plan to get us girls to top it?"

Fuck it, I just came out with it. "First, the losing girl doesn't remove her own clothes, rather the winning guy does, or nominates someone to remove them." I looked at Willow, how was she going to react to this?

She put down her chopsticks and looked at me. "And you'd be OK with that would you Jay? You're not the best player, you'd be OK with Steve removing my bra and running his hands over my breasts?"

Shit, I'd not thought of that. I can be so fucking stupid, all I'd thought about was watching Abi remove her clothes, or watching Willow with her hands inside Susie underwear. It never occurred to me that I'd have to watch Steve holding my girls tits. Fuck.

"You hadn't thought of that had you?"

I shook my head. Willow picked up some rice and ate it, then looked at me again.

"How about then if the winning guy nominates a

girl to remove her clothes?"

I thought about it, I'd be OK with that. "Would you be OK with that Willow?"

Willow laughed, "It was my idea Jay. I think the tricky part would be getting Susie to remove my clothes, don't you?" She was right. Willow continued speaking, "And you said you had a second part to the plan? What was that?"

I swallowed, my mouth had gone very dry.

"As, as last week. The, when we have two naked girls we go to the living room, they get on the mattress and..." my voice failed me.

"Boring, don't you think?"

"No, this time, this time, they, well, go further."

"What do you mean, fuck each other?" I didn't speak, but I must have gone red. "Christ Jay, you do mean fuck each other, don't you?" I nodded, expecting her to storm out, instead I was rather surprised. Willow picked up her beer and emptied it down her neck, then put the empty down.

"I might go along with that," she said softly, "If

the others agree. Two more please," Willow had caught the eye of a waitress and ordered another couple of beers. What a girl!

******

After dinner I walked her home, she had lectures in the morning and her place was much closer to the university than my place. We kissed on the door step, I tried to follow her in but she pushed me away.

"I'm going to think about this Jay," she said, "I won't agree first, but if one or more of the others goes along I'll agree to take part."

We kissed again and parted.

"Are you coming over tomorrow – Jon wants the eight of us to go to the new Greek restaurant."

"Sure, we can discuss it in a group. See you tomorrow." We kissed again and I watched her ass as she walked to the elevator.

"Love you," I shouted. Willow turned and blew me a kiss.

TUESDAY
MARCH 30TH

We walked to work in the morning, the same as any other day. We were stood at the lights, waiting for the 'Walk' sign when Jon spoke.

"So, did you speak to you girlfriends boys? Clearly Mia is up for it, not that she has a choice."

There was silence, so I spoke first.

"Willow will do it, but she had one condition. The winner of the round has to nominate a girl to remove the clothes."

They booed me.

"Guys, best I could manage. Maybe the week after she allow a guy to do it." That hurt me as I said it, I didn't want to watch as one of them fondled my Willow.

"Surprisingly," said Paul, "Abi is game. When I suggested it I half expected her to end with me, but she paused and said OK. I think her repressed lesbian tendencies have come to the fore." Paul started laughing as he ended the sentence. We all joined in as the lights changed and we crossed the street. Smokes was notably quiet.

On the other side of the street, as we pushed open the door to the office he finally broke his silence.

"Susie will agree, I think, but," he took a deep breath, "But, I have to win. If I lose she'll back out."

Suddenly I felt confident. "No."

They all looked at me. "No, if she won't take part you don't get to play." I could barely believe that I'd just been so bold to my friend and landlord, and employer. "Don't get me wrong, we can let you win – not that you'll need much help – but she has to agree to take part. How about if we get them to sign contracts?"

"She won't, well, not this week anyway." Smokes was clearly thinking. "Next week she might, I'll have won five on the trot by then, she'll be very relaxed. But this week, no."

Jon and Paul looked at me, waiting to see where this would go.

"OK bud," I tried to sound confident, "But next week is different."

So it was settled, Willow had a 66% chance of fucking another woman, as I watched. I could feel myself getting a semi as I thought about it. 10 minutes of coding would soon put an end to that.

******

The Greek restaurant (imaginatively known as 'The Greek') is a buffet type place, I don't think you could call it fine dining, but it's as much as you can eat for $15 and the wine is similarly priced. Our table was at the back, nice and out of the way.

"It's you exams next week isn't it?" Smokes asked to no one in particular. All the girls nodded. "How about we have a party on the Saturday at our place?"

Great idea, I'd met Willow at one of our infamous parties. We used to hold them when we were students – it's been a while since we graduated but we still associate with a lot of the University crowd.

"Great idea," said Abi, "Usual rules?"

"Of course." Usual rules, this means no one needs to bring any alcohol, we'll provide it all, as well as food etc. These are great nights. The girls would put the word around and we'll invite some folks from work. Not many though, we might get out of hand and don't want to be reminded on Monday morning.

Between us we were on our fifth bottle (Abi has never forgotten her ID since that fateful night) when the conversation finally got round to Friday's scheduled poker game. Mia spoke first.

"So Willow," she said across the table, making sure that everyone could hear, "Up for a little lesbian action on Friday night?" As soon as she'd finished speaking Mia put a kebab into her mouth and licked the sauce off it, very seductively. But then I knew what she could do with her mouth.

Willow looked at her, the two girls held each other's gaze and no one spoke, waiting for Willow to reply. "I am prepared to Mia, are you?" Mia looked at Jon and then nodded. "And I'm sure you want to go that little bit further, don't you Abi?"

We all looked at Abi, who just blushed, then nodded very gently. Jon must have told Mia to take the lead like this, she's normally so quiet and submissive.

"So that just leaves you Susie," said Mia, not even looking at Susie, "Will you take part?"

Susie swallowed what she was chewing and avoided looking at Mia. "Oh Mia," she said, "I'll enjoy watching you fuck Willow, or Abi." Susie took Smoke's hand and held it, "I mean, it's not like Steve's going to lose, is it."

One day bitch, I thought, one day his luck will run out.

"But if he does," said Abi, "You agree to have full lesbian sex with one of us, while everyone else watches?"

"Of course," said Susie.

"And you'll sign a contract to that effect?" This came from Willow to my surprise.

"Sure," she said, smiling. She had absolute confidence in Smoke's ability to win.

"How about we make it more interesting," said Mia, "Girl in the winning team gets to remove the clothes from the girl in the losing team?" Jon had primed her well and she was a reasonable actress, she didn't look like she was reading from a script. Mind you, I'd had two thirds of a bottle of wine, what did I know?

"Sure," said Susie, "I look forward to removing you clothes Mia."

"Oooh," said Paul, "Fighting talk."

We all laughed at that. The plan had gone better than we had expected. Roll on Friday.

FRIDAY APRIL 3RD

Waking up on Friday is the worst and also the best, the last day of the working week and yet I hate it. When that damn phone beeps I could cheerfully throw it out of the window. Willow was the first to move, she pushed her arm out from under the covers and silenced it.

"Shall I go first," she offered. I just nodded and she slipped out from under the sheets, put my dressing gown on and went for a shower. When she came back she had two cups of coffee and I sipped at it, watching her towel herself. When she caught me watching she threw the towel at me.

"Go for a shower pervert," she laughed. I took the hint (and the towel) and went for a shower. When I came back she was dressed and just putting on some makeup. I started to dress when Willow opened my door.

"I've got to leave now Jay, got a nine am." I checked the clock, she'd be able to walk that in time. I started to dress, Willow stood at the door and watched me.

"Pervert," I said and we both laughed.

"Jay," she said, half out of the door, "Tonight, will you do something for me?"

Fuck, was she insisting that I won? "Sure, I'll try."

"No Jay, I've been thinking about this all week. You'll do something for me tonight."

"OK, what?"

"Make sure you lose." Willow walked through the door and closed it behind her. My mind took a few seconds to register what she'd said. I fell over, half in and half out of my trousers as I made for the door. When I opened it the door to the apartment was just opening, Willow still inside. She looked at me from along the corridor.

"Love you, loser," she said, winked and walked out for the day.

Lose? Sure, I could manage that. How hard could it be?"

******

The four of us were sat in the canteen at lunch, speaking about nothing in particular. In a lull in the conversation I spoke to Smokes.

"Good news for Susie," I said, shoveling some fries into my mouth, "Willow spoke to me on her way out the apartment this morning. She's demanded that I lose."

I looked up, Paul, Jon, Steve, they were all looking at me.

"Say that again bud," said Jon.

"You heard me, she's demanded that I lose. Shouldn't be that hard." I looked at them all, I think they had new found respect for me. Well, respect for Willow anyway.

"Question is," I continued, "Who do you most want to see her fuck?"

"Are you suggesting," said Paul taking a slurp of his

coke, "that we fix the game?"

"Sure," I replied, "one of the losers has already been picked. Why not pick the other?"

We all looked at each other, this was very odd.

"Well," said Jon, "I get to see Mia naked every night – don't get me wrong, I'd love to watch her fuck Willow, but I'd rather see Susie do it. And we've never even seen her tits yet."

Smokes looked up and rubbed his mouth. "Not yet boys, let me win this one, then next time I'll lose, I promise. If I lose this she'd probably go through with it, but I'm pretty certain I'd be single 10 minutes later. But I've got an idea for next week, and I promise I'll lose."

In the end we tossed a coin – Paul wanted to watch Mia and Willow, as did I. Jon and Smokes wanted to watch Abi and Willow. Smokes tossed a coin and I called heads, I watched as it bounced once, then twice on the table before it started to spin. Soon it was clear, Washington was staring up at me. Willow was going to fuck Mia that night.

"One more suggestion," Jon said, "How about we ask the girls to wear sexy cocktail dresses tonight

– then before the losers fuck they get dressed again, so we can watch a longer show as they undress?"

"Good idea," said Paul, "And one more thing, don't lose too fucking quickly. Let's get Abi down to her underwear at least."

We all texted our girlfriends. The afternoon passed very, very slowly.

******

When we got back to the apartment, after the obligatory couple of after work beers, we could see that the lights were on, good. At least one of the girls was already there. We went in and through to the living room, Abi, Susie and Mia were already there. And they looked absolutely stunning, it looked like they'd all been to the same shop.

Mia was wearing a black dress (all three of them had on a black dress) that barely covered her chest and stopped just below her pussy. The dress was tight to her body, armless. She'd clearly been to the hairdressers as well, her long black hair looked incredible.

Abi's dress was off one shoulder and quite low

cut, whatever bra she was wearing was earning it's keep, pushing her toned breasts upwards and out- wards.

But the star was Susie, her dress was over both shoulders and cut a long way down the front, far enough to show that she wasn't wearing a bra. The lower part was on an angle, coming high up her right hip and almost down to her left knee. Fuck, I found myself staring at her. When she noticed she smiled.

"Like what you see Jay?" I just nodded.

We sat down and chatted, waiting for Willow. I really hoped she would have put as much effort in as the other girls. When she arrived I wasn't disappointed. Willow had had her hair styled, it looked like she'd been to the beautician as well, her makeup was better than I'd ever seen from her before – her lips matched her hair color, her eyes looked dark and mysterious. But her dress – wow. When she walked in we all stopped talking and just stared at her. It was tiny, the skirt just below her pussy, split down the front to her belly button, a cord laced up the front holding it together (and holding her breasts in). It went over both shoul- ders, but the material was skimpy over her breasts and revealed a huge amount of side boob. She looked stunning.

Willow walked across the room and sat on the chair arm of the chair I was sat in. When she sat down she slowly crossed her legs, a quick glance showed everyone was watching her. What a girl. My girl.

"So," said Willow, "Are we going to eat something before we play?" I was the first to recover, after some discussion I phoned out for Chinese. We ate in the dining room – normally the boys would all get changed, but seeing as the girls had made so much of an effort we decided to keep our suits on. Hell, we even did our top buttons and donned ties. It made it seem much more real somehow.

To protect the girls' nails, and makeup in general, for once the boys cleaned up and just after eight we sat down to play cards. It was different this time, we were playing for a purpose, to a goal. To make sure that Jon and I lost.

Smokes spoke as he shuffled the cards. "The rules are simple. Dealer picks the game, small blind is $100, big blind $200. Rebuy is $5,000, the price is one item of clothing from the losing girl. Girls to remain silent at all times, unless they want a punishment, in addition to losing an item of clothing. We play until two girls are naked, at which point they both get dressed, then we retire to the living room and they fuck while the rest of us watch. I've prepared contracts to this effect."

Smokes pushed a piece of paper to each couple, we read it and signed. Willow had just agreed that if (when) I lost she would fuck another girl while I watched. After she signed she looked at me and smiled, a knowing smile. She really was looking forward to this. She wasn't the only one.

I lost the first round, fuck I wasn't even trying to, I had a decent hand but Paul had a better one.

"OK," said Paul, "I nominate Susie to remove Willow's shoes," he started simply. Susie looked at Steve who nodded to her. Susie walked round the table and bent down in front of Willow who raised one leg, then the other as Susie removed her black high heels and set them to one side. I took another $5,000 in chips from the bank. Onwards and upwards.

As Willow and Susie weren't wearing bras we agreed that Susie's necklace and the lace tie holding Willow's dress together would count as an item of clothing. In a rare display of crapiness Smokes lost the next round, again to Paul. This time he nominated Abi to remove an item of clothing, Susie had a look of absolute fear on her face. Shit, if Paul picked the dress we'd finally get to see her huge teenage tits. But Paul was a gentleman, he nominated Abi and as she stood behind Susie he told her to remove her necklace. Abi did it very sexily, she unhooked it then took one end in each hand and pushed her hands over Susie's shoulders, just touching the top of Susie's ample chest, before pulling her hands away. This was going to be a great game.

******

After two dozen rounds and several lost items of clothing the score was every girl had lost at least one item of clothing, Mia had lost her shoes and pantyhose. I duly lost the next round (got to keep up with Jon) and Smokes won the round.

"Abi," he said, "Why not remove the cord from Willow's dress?" I liked his choice, fuck we'd get to see Mia doing it later. Abi walked to Willow and lifted her hands.

"Stop," said Paul, "Put your hands behind your back, fold them there." Abi did as she was told. "Now Abi, use your mouth." Abi looked at Paul, then leaned forward to obey. Gently she opened her mouth and tried to take the end of the cord into her mouth, it took her a couple of attempts before she got it into her mouth and she pulled, the bow coming undone. As soon as it did Willow's dress relaxed, the V in the front opening a little wider, her breasts moving slightly to the side. It took Abi another 10 minutes to get the string completely out, but it was 10 minutes well spent. I was pretty hard at the end of it, and looking round the table I wasn't the only one enjoying the show. Next time I lost I think she'd be losing her dress. Well, it would be a bit challenging to remove her panties with it still on!

Abi lost her dress in the next round, to my surprise I won so I had Willow remove it. As with the cord I ordered her to use her mouth, after a few minutes it was obvious that she couldn't undo the zipper so I allowed her to use her hands to pull it down. Once the zipper was down I ordered to put her arms back behind her back and she used her mouth to ease the strap off Abi's shoulder. I loved the way that both girl's tits bounced and moved as they worked together to get the dress to the floor. When it was finally down Abi stepped out of the dress, showing her matching set. Abi kicked it to one side and resumed standing behind Paul. Willow returned to my side.

Over the hours each girl except Susie lost her dress in the same manner. Willow was reduced to just her panties just after 10, Mia was naked by 10:30, Abi was reduced to her underwear at about the same time. All I had to do now was lose one more hand.

Just my luck, I started to get excellent hand after excellent hand. Abi lost her bra, Mia removed it with her hands. She undid it slowly, being strapless if she'd let go it would have fallen straight to the floor but Mia and Abi played to the crowd, Mia held it in place with one hand then slipped her other hand inside the bra, holding Abi's breast before allowing it to fall. Mia then moved her hand and held her nipple, teasing it erect before moving to one side and returning to Jon's side.

Fuck me, next hand and I got a pair of Aces in the hole. Of all the fucking luck. I was tempted to fold, but decided to stay in. In the flop there was another fucking ace, then the river card was an ace. You could play a lifetime and not get four fucking aces.

Smokes filled his lungs with camel smoke and exhaled. "All in," and pushed his chip mountain into the center of the table. This was it.

"Fold," said Jon, dropping out. I looked at Smokes, I should fold. Instead I formed a plan.

"All in," I said, pushing my much smaller chip pile in. Smokes smiled at me.

"Read 'em and weep Jay, Jacks over Aces, full house."

By rights I had him beat. Instead I just looked at him and smiled, "Bastard" I said and pushed my cards into the pile, ensuring that no one could see them. The game was over, I'd played my part. I tried to look hard done by, but who was I kidding?

"Abi, you must be pleased to avoid stripping off," said Smokes, "So why not remove Willow's panties. And yes, use your teeth."

Abi and Willow looked at each other, they exchanged a sly smile. Abi moved to Willow's side, and as Mia had done the previous week eased the panties down over her hips, taking it slowly, allowing them to fall to the floor, exposing her bald pussy. When they were on the floor Willow stepped out, I expected Abi to move back behind Paul, instead she moved to the floor and picked Willow's panties up in her teeth. When she stood up she looked round the room, then moved behind Paul, Willow's black panties hanging from her mouth.

"Well I'll be . . . ." Jon didn't finish his sentence.

"OK boys, see you in the living room. Susie, Abi, care to get dressed and join us? Mia, Willow, see you there soon." We stood up and moved to the living room, Susie and Abi joined us five minutes later, another five minutes later Willow and Mia came in, holding hands, once more back in their little black dresses. We'd put the mattress out while they got dressed, the room was ready for them.

The room fell silent when Willow entered, she was holding Mia's hand and leading her – Willow's taller than Mia so I guess that was why she took the lead. Both girls looked amazing in their tight dresses. When they came into the room they turned to face each other and gave nervous smiles, then took each other's hands and leaned in, Mia went up on her toes a little and Willow bent down as they kissed softly, lips touching as Willow kissed a girl for the first time.

Everyone else watched in silence as their mouths opened and tongues came out. Willow let go of Mia's hands and put them onto Mia's face. In turn Mia put her hands onto Willow's ass and started to stroke it.

Still kissing Mia Willow moved her hands down Mia's neck and down her back, where her fingers found Mia's zipper and she slid the zipper down slowly, before putting her hands inside the shoulder straps and easing them off. The dress came down quickly, revealing Mia's toned body.

I sneaked a quick look around the room, everyone was staring silently as the two girls made out, even stuck up Susie was watching, barely blinking.

When I looked back Willow's dress was coming off, Mia was kissing Willow's neck and Willow had her eyes closed, a hand on Mia's head, guiding her down. Mia pushed the dress off one shoulder and it fell down over Willow's body, revealing her full chest. Mia then reached behind Willow and undid her bra, pulling the straps over her shoulders and down her arms, her breasts falling slightly as the sexy undergarment was removed.

Mia looked up at Willow, they were both smiling and she took Willow's breasts into her hands and held them for a few second, before opening her mouth and kissing each in turn. Willow looked at me and winked, fuck she was enjoying all of this, both Mia's touch and the public attention of the crowd. When Mia sucked one of her nipples she moaned, Willow always had sensitive breasts and nipples but I think that the attention was making it even better for her.

Mia took Willow's hand and walked her to the mattress, fuck they were less than three feet away from me. Willow lay on her back and put her hand onto Mia's head, pushing her down, between her legs. Mia looked up at the crowd and grinned, then put her head back and started to lick Willow's pussy through her panties. The instant her tongue touched the lacy material Willow gasped out loud, followed by a long intake of breath.

Willow's head was almost between my legs, I could have reached down and touched her but I held firm. I wanted to jump on her, force my cock down her throat (and fuck I would have if it wasn't for the other people present, instead I just slipped my hand inside my pants and adjusted my cock. Bet I wasn't the only one.

On the mattress Mia had pulled Willow's panties to one side and was licking on her sweet pussy, Willow was moving on the mattress, her breasts rising and falling as she breathed deeply. Willow put her hands onto her breasts and squeezed them, pushing them together as she got more and more excited. Mia pushed one, then two fingers inside Willow who gasped, it wouldn't be long before she came.

Mia looked round, then formed her tiny hand into

a fist and slowly, ever so slowly pushed it inside Willow's cunt, it took her almost a minute before her hand disappeared inside Willow and then she really started to fist fuck Willow, pushing her hand in and out. Willow was shouting in delight, I'm sure she'd never had anything that big inside her, and she was loving it. Within seconds Willow was begging, pleading for a release. Mia teased her, she could see that all Willow needed was a touch on her clit.

Mia kissed Willow's thighs before finally giving Willow what she needed. As soon as her tongue touched Willow's clit Willow came, screaming loudly, sinking her nails into her own breasts. Normally Willow demands that I stop moving when she cums, allowing her to rest as orgasm engulfs her but Mia didn't let up, she continued to suck Willow's clit and fist fuck her.

"I'm going to cum again, oh fuck I'm going to CUM." Willow screamed the word as she came a second time within 30 seconds, her first orgasm barely having subsided.

Mia gently pulled her hand out of Willow then raised it up to Willow's face. When she opened her eyes Willow took hold of Mia's wrist and she sensually licked her own wetness off Mia's hand. I think both girls had forgotten that anyone else was present.

Willow propped herself up and the girls kissed, then Mia pushed Willow down into the mattress. Mia sat on Willow's chest, her tiny body nestling between Willow's tits. Mia removed her bra, then lifted herself up and lost her panties. They only had eyes for each other.

Mia leaned forward and slid her pussy over Willow's chest and face, leaving a gap of two or three inches. Willow smiled, she was going to have to work for her first taste of pussy. She lifted her head up and took her first taste of another girl. When her tongue touched Mia's pussy Mia threw her head back and moaned, then she lowered her body down, pushing Willow's head down.

Willow put her hands onto Mia's ass, pulling her in as she pushed her tongue along the soft folds of Mia's labia. Fuck, I remembered her taste well. Somehow Willow managed to insert a finger into Mia. Mia was grinding her pussy against Willow's mouth, pushing her pussy up and down, controlling what part of her body Willow was being forced to suck.

Mia put her hands on her head and threw her head back, she was close to cumming – fuck, had Jon given her permission to cum? Would she ask? Mia was begging, pulling her hair with her hand. Mia locked eyes with Jon, very gently he nodded his head and Mia collapsed forward, she'd asked if she should cum and he had granted her permission to do so.

Eventually Mia climbed off Willow and they kissed again, before Mia moved to the middle of the mattress and knelt there, legs together. Willow looked at her and went to kneel next to her lover. Smokes was first to act, he started to clap. Within seconds I joined in, then everyone else did. Willow blushed, Mia just smiled.

Jon stood up first, "If you'll excuse Mia and I." He took Mia's hand and they walked out. Everyone else stood up, Willow and I were last to leave.

I led the naked Willow back to my room, my cock was rock hard (as I suspect were all the boys). As soon as we were inside I closed the door and turned to face Willow.

"Well," she said, "Did you enjoy that? I certainly did."

"Oh God yes," I replied. "That was fucking awesome."

"Just think," she said, walking slowly towards me, "a few weeks ago you said you wanted me to suck Mia's pussy juices off your cock. Instead," she added, putting a finger to my lips, "You get to suck her juices off my face, my fingers . . . ."

I opened my mouth and Willow put her fingers in, wet with Mia's pussy juices inside my mouth and she closed, sucking it gently. Ah, it brought back memories.

Abruptly Willow pulled her hand out and dropped to her knees, taking my cock into her mouth and sucking it, I was already rock hard, well, how wouldn't I be having watched my girl-friend fucking another girl two feet away from me?

Willow only sucked me for a few seconds before she moved again, getting onto the bed, lying on her back, her head hanging off the edge of the bed. She didn't speak, just looked at me and started to finger fuck herself. I knew what she wanted.

I got out of my clothes as fast as I could, moved towards her and dropped to my knees. Willow opened her mouth and I thrust my hard cock straight in, this wasn't a blowjob, this was a face fuck, and we were both going to enjoy it.

Willow gagged as I used her mouth, bucking my hips as I fucked her face. I put my hands onto her tits, crushing them in my hands, down her body I could she her hands moving quickly over her clit as she tried to cum again – three times on one night, greedy girl.

Saliva was running down her face, into her eyes and hair. I wasn't thinking of her at all, just fucking her for all I was worth. Must have been how excited she was as soon Willow stopped gagging and for the first time ever I pushed all the way to the back of her throat, I felt it open and the end of my cock disappeared into her throat. Holy shit, this was an unreal sensation.

I slowed, wanting to enjoy the sensation, I pulled out and Willow spoke to me.

"Put it back Jay, keep your cock there, choke me with it."

I waited till she took a deep breath then did as she ordered and pushed, once more feeling her throat open wide and accept my cock. I couldn't believe the sensation for me – and Willow, her hand was moving incredibly fast as she rubbed her clit. After a while I could see her chest rising and falling, she was bucking on the bed, trying to draw in breath.

I pulled back a little, her left hand moved quickly onto my ass, pulling my back in and then her hand slowed, her hips lifted, back arched and I could feel her trying to control her jaws as she came. Even then she didn't let go of my ass, holding me in place for another 15 seconds or so until finally she let go and I pulled out, instantly Willow drank in the air. I allowed her to breathe out and in three times before I reinserted my cock, once more beyond her gag point and I thrusted very gently, only moving a quarter inch or so, just the tip of my cock moving in her throat.

It only took me a few seconds before I started to shoot cum down her throat, pumping my load down. I yelled out as I came, knowing how deep my cock was intensified my orgasm. I stayed where I was after I came, only pulling out when Willow slapped my ass to show me she couldn't take it any longer and needed to breathe.

When I pulled out I fell onto the bed next to her, Willow was drinking in the air, she rolled over next to me and hugged me.

"That was an amazing night Jay," she said, "I loved sex with Mia."

Me too, I thought. Shit, stop thinking that in case I say it out loud. I kissed her and turned out the light and we went to sleep.

SATURDAY
APRIL 4TH

I woke late, Willow was still fast asleep so I left her in bed, I slipped out without waking her, put on my dressing gown and went to the kitchen. As usual, there was hot coffee on the go. Unusually all the boys were in there, sat round the table, chatting. There weren't any girls. As I walked in they all cheered.

"Hero of the hour!" They raised their cups to me in a salute.

"Surely Willow was the hero," I said.

"Mate," said Smokes, "You got her to perform, you're the real hero."

I sat down and smiled, I'd never been the hero before. It felt good.

We talked aimlessly, when the conversation went

silent Smokes, naturally, broke the silence.

"Boys, I know how we can top that." We looked at him expectantly, but at that point we could hear footsteps. "We'll discuss on Monday."

"Morning," said Abi as she walked into the room. We changed the subject.

MONDAY
APRIL 6TH

"So," said Jon, chasing the piece of chicken round his plate, "What's you're big plan for this Friday?" He looked at Steve. There's no smoking at work, not even for the boss' son. It seems odd talking to Steve without him puffing away on a Camel.

"Well," said Steve, "How about for this Friday the losing girl becomes the winner's slave for the weekend?"

We all looked at each other. Was he serious?

"And, given last week I'll make a genuine offer. I'll lose. So the game is between the three of you. Winner gets Susie for the weekend, from game end until eight am Monday." He said with an almost total lack of emotion.

We were all silent, thinking about it. Eventually I

broke the silence.

"Will she go for it?" I asked.

"Boys, she has total faith in my ability to win. So, yes. We'll get her to sign a contract, all of the girls, to that effect. I don't think you're girlfriends will object, will they?"

I thought about it, Willow had become pretty damn submissive over the last few weeks, fuck she'd even worn a makeshift collar and called me sir. Yes, Willow would go for it, especially if she knew she wasn't going to be enslaved.

"Well Mia's up for it, obviously," said Jon.

"Abi can't stop talking about her and Mia, and then Willow and Mia. Yes, I think she can be persuaded," added Paul

"Willow will do it." I was 99% certain.

Steve stood up and picked up his tray. "Let's discuss tomorrow, talk to your girls tonight and we can take it from there."

******

"Are you serious? Are you fucking serious? There is no fucking way I will be a slave girl to any of the other guys. What the fuck were you thinking?" Willow shouted at me. 99% now seemed a long way away.

"Wait, Willow, wait, let me finish." She paused, she was still furious but she paused.

"This had better be good."

"Steve is going to lose."

Willow looked at me, then put her head back and laughed. "Really? We get to see Susie humiliated?" I nodded. In the space of 30 seconds she had gone from normal, to furious like I'd never seen her, to a look of satisfaction.

"So, if you win, we get to own Susie for the weekend?" Willow was now calm and plotting, I could see it in her face. She'd never really got on with Susie, the idea of being able to control and dominate her was clearly very appealing.

Willow dropped to her knees and pulled my cock out of my boxers. She took it into her mouth and sucked for a while, as soon as I was fully hard she popped it out and wanked me, looking up at my face.

"Will you make her suck your cock sir?"

"Yes."

"And will I have to watch as she sucks you sir?" I nodded. "Will you make her suck my pussy sir?" I nodded again." Willow put a hand into her panties, as soon as she touched herself she gasped.

"And will I be able to command her sir?"

"Yes."

Willow panted, her hand was moving quickly inside her panties. She smiled and took me back into her mouth, she only sucked me for another minute before she took me out again.

"Can I cum sir? Please sir, tell me you'll make Susie beg like this ... make her beg like me sir ..." Fuck I wanted to let Willow cum, but this was took much fun.

"Work for it Willow, beg for it."

"Let me ... please let me cum sir ... please ..."

"I'll count to 10 slave. Then you can cum." Slave, I'd called her that once before. She didn't flinch.

"One . . . two . . . three . . . four" With each number she was more and more excited, I could see that she was struggling to contain herself, she was moaning ever louder and gently begging for a release. Fuck I was tempted to stop counting at eight to tease her. But not today.

Willow had her other hand on one of her breasts, squeezing it through the material of her blouse. She was making high pitched noises, her breathing was fast and shallow as I counted higher. I slowed down at six, waiting a full five seconds before getting to seven. She must have been thinking I would never get to ten.

"eight ...... nine .... ten."

Willow collapsed onto the floor, her head hitting my foot as she came, screaming loudly, she was thanking God for her orgasm. She wrapped one arm round my legs, her body was writhing on the floor as she continued to cum. When she finally stopped cumming and breathed normally she looked up at me.

"I really hope you win on Friday sir, I was thinking about sitting on Susie's face as I masturbated." Willow got back onto her knees and looked up at me. "Now, about that blowjob sir." She took me back into her mouth and sucked.

No challenge then for Friday, I just had to win. The thought of having Susie and Willow together should spur me on. Mind you, it would spur on everyone else as well.

WEDNESDAY APRIL 8TH

"Right," said Jon, "I've drawn the contract up for Friday's game, have a read, see what you think." I'm no expert in this, I read it and it seemed pretty comprehensive. Each couple would sign, the losing girl would become the property of the winning man for the weekend, starting at the end of the game, ending at 8am Monday morning. She would exist without rights, agreed to accept any punishment. She would not be permanently damaged (well physically, I knew what Steve had planned for her at the party – she would be carrying a few mental scars).

"Seems OK," said Steve.

"Sure? Susie's going to be the one losing."

Steve just inhaled on his camel and smiled. "She won't like it boys, but she'll do it. Besides Jon, I see what you have with Mia, I can't stop thinking about it. I want that. I'd like Susie to be my slave, but if not her I'll find another one. Can't be that hard, not if you've managed it." Steve was smiling when he said this.

This is America, the second or third thing you get asked on a date is 'So what do you do?' Hi I'm a computer programmer isn't the best line. On the other hand, hi, I'm a multi-millionaire and one day will run the company works pretty well. Yep, he'd have no problems picking up a girl to be his slave. I want to hate him, I really do.

"Fuck you," replied Jon, also smiling.

Fuck, I wanted what Jon had as well. Willow was being pretty submissive, but not submissive enough. I had to keep working on her.

THURSDAY
APRIL 8TH

"I've got an idea for the party," said Steve to me over lunch. Jon and Paul were running late, so there was just the two of us.

"I'm all ears."

"If you agree to it I'll do my best to make sure you win, can't guarantee it, but I'll try my hardest."

"Go on," I replied, I had no idea what he was going to suggest.

"Well, it's like this..."

FRIDAY APRIL 10TH

We sat down to play cards. Behind each of us, over our left shoulder were our girlfriends. Each of them look amazing. Susie looked especially good, her long blonde hair cascading over her shoulders, offsetting her black dress. Steve looked round and pulled out the game contract. He took out his pen and signed it, then Susie signed. She looked round the whole table with a superior air, like someone who was going to win and she knew it.

Steve passed the contract to Jon and Mia who signed before passing it to me. I made a show of reading it (along with Willow) before we signed, then Paul and Abi signed. We were ready. Steve spoke.

"To be clear, at the end of the game the loser is the first girl with no clothes and her partner has no money. The winner is the couple with the most money. Each item of clothing is valued at $5,000 and that value will be added to the money total. Any questions?"

We all shook our heads.

"Round winner removes (or nominates someone to remove) the re-buy item of clothing. Any girl speaks she will be punished, a taste of what's to come if she's on the losing team, if you will." All the boys smiled as he said this, the girls looked slightly worried – even Susie.

"Before we start," said Jon reaching under the table, "Let me put this out there." He lifted up a slave collar and a leash. He put them onto the middle of the table. I looked round, each girl was staring at it, and suddenly it was very real for them.

"Right, let's play cards."

******

I won't bore you with the early rounds. It all went to play, Steve was making sure that he lost, the rest of us were playing for real. I suspect he was folding when he had good hands and betting when he didn't. Anyway, after a couple of hours the position, clothes wise, was this. Susie was wearing her bra, panties, stocking and suspenders. She'd never been this naked before. Smokes had a few thousand dollars left. Susie looked worried.

Behind me Willow had only lost her shoes, Mia was as undressed as Susie. Paul was playing out of his skin, Abi was still fully clothed. But he was out of this round – Abi might have all her clothes but I had the most chips. I turned over my cards to show Smokes.

"Fuck," said Smokes, "Fuck you man!" His face broke into a broad grin as he said the words. Behind him Susie looked worried.

"Please," she said, "please . . . I, I don't want," her voice trailed out. As the winner the honor was mine. I stood up and walked round the table until I was behind Susie. She was a good girl, she didn't move, her arms folded behind her back. I unhooked her bra and looked across at Willow, my girl, still in her skirt, arms folded the same way. She smiled at me, she wanted to see this as well.

I slipped my hands inside Susie's bra and eased it over her shoulders, down her arms. Smokes moved on his chair to watch. Everyone's eyes were on Susie and my hands. I moved my hands over her shoulders, down her chest. I crossed them over and pushed my hands into her bra.

Susie pushed her head back, closing her eyes. Her protests had died in her mouth. I squeezed her huge breasts inside their container before pushing it down her body. When her tits were free I removed my hands to shouts from Paul and Jay, Mia Willow and Abi were all smiling (the girls remembering not to make any noise). Susie had spoken, she'd be punished for that once her bra was off.

I moved my hands back up her body, taking her tits back into my hands for a second squeeze, then over her shoulders to her arms. I moved them, allowing her bra to fall to the floor, before moving back to my seat.

"You spoke Susie," said Smokes without looking at her, "What should happen now?"

Susie didn't answer for a few seconds, when she spoke she had tears in her eyes. "I should be punished Sir."

"Yes, yes you should. Walk around the table and offer your tits to everyone for punishment, girls as well."

"Yes Sir," she replied. What else could she say? She set off slowly, trying to delay the inevitable. First stop was with Jon and Mia. Barely able to speak she bent down to Jon.

"Would you like to punish my tits sir?"

"Fuck yes," replied Jon, a massive smile on his face.

Susie was shaking, her huge teenage breasts just inches from Jon's face. He opened his hands and raised them up. He brought them down and paused, just before slapping her tits. Poor Susie, she couldn't help it and she pulled back, involuntarily. Steve slapped her ass.

"Behave and keep still."

"I'm sorry Sir," she said, tears forming in her eyes. This time she managed to stand still as Jon slapped her firm tits. The sound reverberated round the room and Susie gasped in pain. She'd taken the punishment as the rules demanded. Next she walked to me. She managed to speak through her tears.

"Would you like to punish my tits sir?"

I looked at Willow who nodded. Her tits were almost level with my face. I reached up and took them into my hands, before taking her nipples between my thumb and forefinger. Without warning I squeezed them hard, then twisted, inflicting what I imagined to be considerable pain on her – judging by the way she screamed I wasn't wrong. The tears continued to flow down her face, her legs were wobbling now as she walked to Paul. I almost felt sorry for her as she stammered the words out to Paul.

"Would you like to punish my tits sir?"

Interestingly, Paul didn't look at Abi for permission. I could see red marks forming on Susie's tits from where Jon had struck her. Would Paul go easy on her? Nope, once, twice, three times he raised his arms and brought his hands down into her already red flesh. Smokes must have been proud of her, despite her tears, shaking and screaming she didn't pull away. When Paul turned away she went back to stand behind Smokes. I ignored her for a moment, then spoke.

"Haven't you got something you'd like to say to Steven?"

"Would . . . would you . . . sir, would you like to punish my tits?"

Would Smokes have the balls? This could well be

the end of his relationship, depending on what he said or did. Mind you, he'd just allowed Susie to be punished, maybe it was all over already.

Smokes lived up to his name, rather than do anything he picked up his camel and filled his lungs with nicotine. He slowly turned to Susie and held the smoking end of his cigarette, pushing the red hot burning end towards her nipple. I was rapt, I couldn't take my eyes off. Surely he wasn't about to push the end of his cigarette into her nipple.

Susie's eyes were wide open, she was shaking almost uncontrollably as the end got closer and closer. I couldn't believe that she stayed still, I'd never seen anyone that scared. When the end was half an inch away from her nipple Smokes laughed and pulled the camel back, putting the end in his mouth and smoking.

"No, she's suffered enough. Won't speak again though, will you?" He didn't look but behind him Susie just shook her head.

Next to lose clothing was Mia, then Abi, then Susie again. This time Paul won the round and he looked at Susie. She'd calmed down but it was time for her to lose her stockings.

"Mia, Abi, work together, mouths only please and remove Susie's stockings and suspenders." Both girls nodded and walked round, got onto their knees and took the lacy material into their mouths. They worked together, pulling the suspender belt down, over Susie's hips and let it fall, until her stockings were holding the suspender belt up around her knees. They then took it back into their mouths and pulled, her stockings coming down her long waxed legs until they were on the floor. Susie then stepped out and kicked them to one side. She looked amazing, her long blonde hair down her back, her full, firm teenage chest a curious mix of creamy white flesh and bright red marks from where she'd been hit. Looking at her, I think she was resigned to her fate – only her panties to go.

Smokes picked up the cards and shuffled. "Well," he said, "I had to lose one day. Seven card stud boys, nothing wild." He dealt out the cards, two for each of us while I put in the big blind. I picked my hand up and looked at them. This was it, this was the big one. Ace of spades and ace of hearts. I put my cards down and picked up my beer, hoping beyond hope that I didn't look anywhere near as excited as I was.

Paul passed, as did I. Jon looked at us both, then

put in a thousand dollars. Smokes, as usual, in-haled before matching the bet. Paul folded and I called. This was going to be a big round. Smokes burnt the top card and then dealt out four cards into the middle, face down. Slowly, ever so slowly he turned them over. Fuck, another ace, then a jack, a four and a ten.

"Your bet Jay," said Steve.

I tried to be nonchalant, but probably just came over as drunk as I pushed another $2,000 into the pot. Jon watched me then laughed, he called. Bet was with Steve.

"I see your $2,000," he said, "and raise you $2,000."

That was it, every dollar of his was in the pot. If either Jon or I beat him Susie was losing her last item of clothing and would be a slave for the weekend. I had to bet, I wasn't sure if Paul would win, Abi had only lost one item of clothing but he had fewer chips than me or Jon. It was going to be close.

"Fuck, fuck," I said and pushed in $2,000 to call. This was going to be it.

"Call," added Jon, pushing in his $2,000.

Smokes inhaled two more lungfuls, before speaking. "Well, well." He put his cigarette into the ashtray, the leaned back and put his arm round Susie's ass. He held it for a moment then laughed.

"OK, let's do it." He slowly burnt the top card and pushed a card to each of us. Oh yes, a four in the hole. A full house. Surely I was going to win?

I looked round the table and smiled, before putting my cards down.

"Full house boys, Aces over fours."

"Fuck," said Jon. He didn't show his cards, just threw them at Smokes. We all looked at Smokes. He smiled before picking up his cards. We stared at each other, he picked up his cards. He blew out the smoke he was holding in his lungs.

"Well, I've got ..." he tapped his cards on the table, "I've got ..." he threw his cards into the center, "Fuck all. Fuck." Behind him Susie started to shake again, she knew what was coming.

"Question is," said Smokes as he slapped Susie's

ass, "Who gets to own you for the weekend?" As he said own Susie shook again. That made it real.

"Don't look at me boys," said Jon, "It's between you two." I looked at Paul and we both laughed, we counted our chips and added up the value of clothing. I couldn't help it, I laughed like a drain, I'd won by $600. Susie was mine, I owned her as a slave. I looked around the table, everyone was smiling. Well, everyone except Susie.

"Come here slave."

Susie started to walk. "Stop," I said. Susie stopped. "I gave you and order, you say 'Yes Master' then obey. OK?" Susie nodded, took a half step, then looked at me.

"Yes master," she said very quietly. As she walked I spoke to her again.

"You will obey every order from me and address me as Master. You will address the other men as sir and obey their orders, as long as they don't counteract mine. You will address Abi, Willow and Mia as mistress and obey their orders, as long as they don't counteract mine or one of the boys. Understand?"

"Yes master."

When she was along side Willow I picked up the collar and chain and looked at her.

"In the absence of any instructions you will spend your time on your knees." As she started to move I spoke again, "But first remove your panties."

"Yes master," she said, pulling them off and then dropping to the floor. Nice, her cunt was freshly waxed, hair free. When she was on her knees I invited everyone else to stand round. I opened the collar and leaned over her.

"Willow," I said, "Lift her hair up." Willow took handfuls of her hair and lifted it out of the way of Susie's neck. I leaned in and put the thick leather collar round her neck. It was adjustable and I fitted it tight, but not so tight that she'd struggle to breathe. I picked up the two padlocks and fitted them, locking the collar in place. As the last one went on Smokes started to clap, then everyone joined in. Susie tried to put on a brave face, but she just looked scared.

"From now on your name is Slave, understand?"

"Yes master."

"Open your legs wide, wider. That's it. Put your hands on your thighs. That's it slave. This is now your default position." We were all staring as she moved gracefully into position.

"Shall we go to the living room?" said Abi.

"Sure. Clean up slave, then come to join us." My cock was growing in my pants, Susie, no Slave was looking good. And I'd be fucking her very soon. So would Willow. As I stood up last I was last out of the room, well, Willow was just behind me. She kissed my neck as we left the room.

"Well done sir," she said quietly. I don't think anyone else heard her.

Behind me I heard Slave standing up. I looked into the room, it wouldn't take her long to clean up.

******

15 minutes later Slave came back into the living room. I was sat in a chair, Willow on the arm. All the girls had got dressed again. We all stopped speaking as she crossed the room, then as defiantly

as she could Slave sank to her knees, opened her legs and put her hands on her thighs as she'd been trained. Everyone was looking at her, I stole a glance at Mia who caught my eye and winked, she was approving of my first steps with Susie.

Smokes broke the tension. He held out his beer, it was empty. "Get me another one Slave."

Slave looked up at me and I nodded. "Yes sir," she said, getting up and walking out of the room.

"Fuck," said Smokes and we all laughed. She was going to do this. Not that she had a choice

******

We sat drinking and chatting until just before one am. We all ordered Susie around, making her put away the empties, getting us replacement beers or something to eat when we felt hungry. When I needed to piss I desperately wanted to piss down her throat, like I had with Mia but I thought that that would be a step too far – not only for Susie, I didn't think Steve would allow it either. Even in my drunken state I could see it would be too much. Instead I decided to put another item I'd done with Mia into practice.

"Slave, clean up the room, then come back here."

"Yes Master," Susie replied, getting up off the floor. We all watched her clean the empties away and generally tidy round. Once it was clean she came back and was about to get to her knees.

"Slave, get on all fours."

"Yes Master," she said and dropped to her hands and knees.

Smokes stood up. "Looks like it's bed time for me. All on my own."

"Wait," I replied, "I've got an idea. Mia, I don't suppose your riding crop is here, is it?" We all knew that Mia liked to ride horses (and be ridden).

She looked at Jon who nodded, almost unperceivably. He'd guessed what was coming. "Could you get it please?"

"Sure."

Mia was gone for a few minutes, I could see that everyone wanted to ask me what was going on, but at the same time wanted to wait. When she came back she gave me the crop. I swished it in the air, then offered it to Smokes.

"Why not ride Susie back to your room?" I said.

For once Steve was speechless. He just looked at me.

"Sit on her back, lift your feet up and whip the pony as she takes you back to your room." Steve face broke into a big smile.

"You kinky bastard," he said, "I'd never have thought of that." Yeah, well neither would I, thanks Mia I thought.

Steve sat on Susie's back, she groaned a little as she took his full weight. Steve lifted his legs up and I put his ankles over the backs of her knees, so that his full weight was on her back. Steve looked at me, then brought the crop down onto Susie's ass. She made a noise of pain, then started to crawl slowly, out of the living room and down the corridor. We all watched her ass, her pussy on full display as she crawled away.

"Crawl back when you've delivered Steve to his room," I shouted. When she was no longer visible we all laughed.

"Anyone else want a pony ride?" I asked. It took nearly 20 minutes for poor Susie to ferry everyone back to their room, we could hear the sound of the crop being used and Susie's whining as it was used more and more frequently, until there was only Willow and I left. I could see the fear on Susie's face, I'm so much heavier than anyone else, she wasn't looking forward to carrying me.

"Are you enjoying being a pony?" I asked Susie.

She considered her response before saying it, no doubt fearing giving the wrong answer. In the end she came down on the side of truth.

"No Master," she said.

Willow bent down and put her hand over Susie's ass and onto her pussy. Susie gasped as Willow ran her fingers over Susie's labia and pushed a finger into her cunt. When she pulled it out she showed her finger to me.

"Your slave was lying sir," she said, "Look how wet the slut is." Willow dropped to her knees and showed Susie her finger, covered in Susie's own juices. Willow held it out to Susie, whose face flushed with shame, having been revealed for the slut she was. Willow pushed it closer and closer until Susie opened her mouth and took Willow's finger in and sucked her own wetness off it. I could sense her utter shame.

"Do you want to ride your pony back to our room sir?" Said Willow. Shit, I'd just noticed, Willow was calling me sir.

"No, you can." Willow moved to sit on Susie, but I motioned her to stop. "Why not ride her naked Willow?" Willow gave me a coy smile, she didn't speak, just reached behind her back and unzipped her dress, allowing it to puddle round her ankles. Her bra and panties soon joined them, she was about to remove her suspenders, stockings and shoes when I asked her to leave them on.

"You look so sexy in them," I told her. We stood in front of pony girl Susie, naked, red ass from where the crop had been used. Willow, who six weeks ago was so reserved in public was now almost naked in front of another girl. We kissed passionately as Susie watched from her position on the floor. Eventually we broke off and Willow spoke.

"Take me back your room sir," she said. Willow straddled Susie and then lowered herself onto Susie's back, sitting herself on her hips. I handed her the riding crop and she smiled, then lashed Susie who cried out.

"Walk on whore," she said. Interesting – Willow was submitting to me, but she was enjoying dominating Susie. This was going to make for a great evening. I picked up Willow's clothes and walked beside her. My room was furthest from the living room, we talked as we walked/rode our way back.

"So," said Willow, "Where did you get the idea for this from sir?"

Fuck, I hadn't thought of that. "A video I saw a long time ago," I replied. I was slightly behind Willow, she couldn't see my face which was just as well, I was probably going red. Ahead of us was Jon's room, the door opened slightly and Mia came out – she was facing away from us and hadn't noticed us coming. When she turned round she paused, she was as naked as the other two girls. She didn't speak, just walked past us heading to the bathroom. Willow turned and looked at me, we both laughed. Six weeks ago this just couldn't have happened.

I opened the door to my room and Willow rode Susie in. When she got off Susie rocked back onto her knees and posed, looking round the room. I don't think she'd ever been in there before. I closed the door and went to sit on the bed, to remove my clothes. Willow raised up the crop and brought it down into Susie's back.

"Dumb cunt," she yelled at Susie, "Why aren't you helping your master get undressed?"

"I, I'm sorry Willow OWWWWW", Susie cried out, Willow had lashed her again.

"You call me mistress, remember cunt?"

"Yes mistress, sorry mistress. I'm sorry, I'll help." Willow looked at me and winked, she was enjoying dominating Susie. Susie crawled to me and I lay back on the bed. I raised my feet up so she could remove my shoes. Next she peeled my socks off, then raised herself up to remove my pants. I moved a bit to help her, all I had on was my shirt.

"Why isn't you owner's cock in your mouth slut?" asked Willow. Susie didn't speak, neither did I, fuck my girlfriend had just asked another woman to suck my cock. Could life get any better? A quick strike with the whip to Susie's back got her to move and take me into her mouth.

I'll be honest, I wasn't expecting much and I wasn't disappointed. Susie managed to get two inches into her mouth and that was it. Willow moved to the side so she could watch as Susie sucked my cock, badly. Fuck, having her do it made me realize how much effort Willow had put into learning how to do this in the last few weeks.

Willow looked at me and spoke, "Would you like me to help blow you sir?" I didn't speak, that was a stupid question. Would I like two girls sucking my cock? Fuck, who wouldn't? Willow smiled at me, I had expected her to start licking my balls or something like that, instead she put a hand on the back of Susie's head and pushed. Susie gagged instantly as another couple of inches of my cock disappeared into Susie's mouth. She pulled back and turned her head to the side, coughing and spluttering, slobber falling from her mouth to the floor. When she recovered she turned back.

"I'll show you how to do it slave," said Willow. She pushed Susie out of the way and took me into her mouth. Susie watched, her mouth falling open as Willow forced her head all the way down, every inch of my cock going into her throat. When the tip of my cock reached the back of her mouth, to the gag point she gagged a little but didn't pull back. Instead she rode it out, then kept going until her lips were touching my pubes. It was incredible, she'd never managed to get my full length in. She must have been practicing.

She held me there for 20 seconds or so before pulling back off and out. Willow turned to Susie and smiled, the inference was clear, this is what a real girlfriend trains herself to do.

"Work on me girls," I said, lying back on the bed.

"Slave, lick his asshole."

I didn't need to move, I knew what would happen.

"I will not," said Susie, definitely.

"Oh yes you will Slave," replied Willow. I sat back up and looked at the girls, Susie was shaking slightly.

"Please," she managed to stutter, "Please don't make me do this."

I got off the bed and ordered Susie to lie on her back. I straddled her stomach and pinned her arms under my legs. She looked terrified, and rightly so. Willow handed me the riding crop but I declined it.

"Willow, sit on her face," I ordered Willow.

"My pleasure sir," she replied.

"And Willow, use the crop on her tits, hard as you like." I looked at Susie, she was really scared now. The tone of my voice hardened. "And now Willow will whip your tits until you beg to suck my ass. Assuming anyone can hear you as you eat Willow's pussy."

Susie started to beg, I think she was begging for me to let her go, not have her be forced to eat pussy, to not be whipped. But I couldn't really hear, Willow sank down onto her face and sat there. After a few seconds Willow lashed the crop down onto one of Susie's breasts. She yelped in pain but still didn't take the hint, she was struggling and trying to escape but I must be twice her weight – there was no way she was going to escape. Willow had to hit her three more times until it sank in that her only way out was to start licking.

Willow had the crop up high, but she just lowered it down, her face changed from one of domination to one of relaxed pleasure as Susie started on her first lesbian experience. I watched, I love watching lesbians, but to watch this was a real pleasure. I'd happily have paid. Willow let go of the crop and instead grabbed her own breasts, squeezing them as Susie stuck to eating Willow. I wanked myself slowly, I'd have a job not cumming. I wasn't ready to cum, not yet.

Willow gyrated her hips, allowing Susie to breathe. I half expected Susie to stop licking when Willow lifted up, but she raised her head, following Willow. Willow was soon panting, gasping as she got close to cumming. Willow took her hands off her breasts and instead grasped Susie's, squeezing them tight, sinking her long nails into the tender red flesh.

"Can I cum please sir," asked Willow. She wanted it more than that, I ignored her request. "Please sir, can I cum?" Her pitch was rising and she continued to beg, I watched her fingers as she gripped Susie's tits harder and harder.

"Please . . . Oh God please . . . PLEASE let me CUM sir . . ."

"You can cum Willow," I said. Instantly she fell forward as she came, she couldn't keep herself upright, I caught her as she fell and helped her down gently, putting my cock into her mouth. Willow was still cumming but she started to suck my cock, I could feel her jaws twitching as tried not to bite in her excitement.

When she rolled off she kept my cock in her mouth. I looked at Susie.

"Anything you'd like to say?" I picked up the crop as I asked her. Susie stared at the end of it, transfixed as I swished the air. Quickly she spoke in a soft, nervous voice.

"Please may I suck your asshole sir."

"Very well, seeing as you asked so nicely." I grabbed Willow's hair and pulled her off my cock, then I got onto the edge of the bed and lay back. Willow went to one side and sucked my cock, Susie got between my legs and nervously licked my ass, she wasn't trying hard but I didn't push it. I loved the sensation of having one girl on my cock and another sucking my ass. Only thing that could make it better would be a third girl to kiss and fondle her tits. Maybe one day.

I lay there in heaven, the sensations were incredible and if I'd been sober I'd have cum in seconds. As it was I could lie there for ages, loving the attentions of the two girls. Despite it all they couldn't get me off. When I sat up I looked at them both, Susie looked terrified, Willow quizzical.

"Get on the bed slave," I ordered her, "On your back, legs apart. I'm going for a piss, when I get back I want to see you in a 69 position girls." I didn't wait for an answer and left the room. When I came back they'd done as I asked, I pulled Susie down the bed by her ankles until her pussy was just on the edge of the bed, leaving Willow further back on the bed.

I didn't go in for any foreplay, I just climbed on top and pushed my cock straight inside her and started to fuck – despite what she may have said her cunt was soaking, she'd clearly enjoyed some aspect of getting Willow off. I don't know if she was tensing but her pussy was incredibly tight, she felt great. I looked at Willow who was watching, she should be involved.

I pulled out of Susie and rolled her onto her side, then moved myself behind her into the spoons position. I pushed inside her again, Susie gasped. I lifted Susie, sliding one of my arms under her, the other over her so I could hold both of her tits. Willow moved in and started to kiss Susie, who didn't resist. She was learning. I fucked her hard, her cunt was really tight.

"Go down on Slave, Willow," I ordered. Much as I was enjoying watching the girls kiss I wanted

Susie to cum, so she could be further degraded by cumming when she was being fucked against her will.

"Thank you sir," said Willow. I hadn't expected that, looked like Willow was really enjoying submitting to my control. She moved quickly, as soon as the girls stopped kissing I took one hand off Susie's breast and put it on her face, bending her head towards mine so we could kiss. Susie was panting and breathing quickly, I felt Willow's face against my cock as she started to lick Susie's clit. Susie's hands were opening and closing quickly, despite everything I'd done to her she was going to cum.

She broke off from kissing me and started to beg for permission to cum as I thrust in and out of her.

"Please let me cum master . . . please master . . . Master . . . Master please . . . PLEASE MASTER" Poor girl was screaming to be allowed a release before I finally gave in and granted her permission. I'd timed it well, Susie came instantly, screaming loudly as wave after wave of orgasm spread across her body. I couldn't help it, I came inside her at the same time, pumping load after load of salty cum inside her tight cunt.

When I pulled out Willow moved and instantly

took me in her mouth. I rolled onto my back and pulled Susie close. She draped an arm over me and kissed me.

"Thank you for allowing me to cum master," she said. I was surprised she volunteered this statement, she sounded embarrassed to be thanking me for being allowed to cum. Perhaps understandably.

"Perform better next time slave and you won't get whipped before."

"Yes master," she replied. I could see she was confused by her feelings, on the one hand ashamed and embarrassed that she was thanking a man who'd had her beaten (and let's face it, pretty much raped her), on the other loving the sensation of submitting to me.

"Suck my cock until I'm asleep Willow."

"Yes sir," came back her voice from under the covers. I closed my eyes and went to sleep.

SATURDAY
APRIL 11TH

I woke first, on one side of me Willow lay there, one arm draped over my chest, her hand extending onto Susie's shoulder, who was lying on her side on my other arm. What a way to go to sleep with my cock buried in a willing girl's mouth? What a way to wake up, two sexy girls, one on each arm. I squeezed my arms gently, waking both of them.

"Morning girls."

"Good morning sir/master" they replied. Good to see that Willow was sticking with her submissive role. Come to think of it, good to see that Susie was staying the course. Maybe she'd change her mind later on, but for now life was good. And what better way to start the morning than with a blowjob?

I rolled onto my side to face Willow. We started

to kiss, behind me I felt breath on my neck as Susie started to kiss the back of my neck. She worked across my shoulders and down my back, I loved the feeling of two girls working me. Surely there couldn't be anything better (three girls maybe?).

"Blow me," I ordered Willow. She kissed me once more then disappeared under the sheets, taking me into her mouth. My cock was already semi hard and would soon be fully erect. Susie got up onto one arm and leaned over me, her tits touching my shoulder as she tried to kiss me.

"And you," I said to her, "you can suck my asshole. And no arguing like last night."

Poor Susie, she went grey instantly. I think if it wasn't for the caning she took last night she would have refused. Even so I had to ask a second time.

"Suck my ass. Or I'll cane you and then you can suck my asshole. Remember last night?"

She shivered and quietly said Yes Master, then slipped down under the covers. It took her a long time to work her way to my ass, but there was no way I was going to allow myself to cum before she got there, despite Willow's efforts.

I just lay on my side, lost under the attentions of the two girls. After a slow start Susie got into position and jammed her tongue into my ass. This was every bit as good as last night, no better, I wasn't drunk and could just lie there, loving the sensation of Willow sucking me as Susie licked my ass. The sensation was incredible and it hardly took any time before I put my hands onto Willow's head and bucked my hips, fucking her face. Willow did well, she gagged and spluttered but didn't pull away. Even Susie tried hard, her head moved in time with my hips as she tongue fucked me.

"I'm going to cum, oh fuck I'm cumming slaves," I shouted in delight as my balls tightened and I started to fill Willow's mouth with my salty cum. I held her there, not allowing her to pull off as my cock continued to twitch in her mouth. When I finally decided to release her I said

"Don't swallow, not yet anyway Willow."

I pulled her up by her hair and looked at her. She smiled, pleased at what she'd done. I reached behind me and grabbed Susie's hair, she was still dutifully licking my ass but I'd had enough now. When she came up I ordered the two girls to kiss, to share the sperm.

"Please, no, don't make me do this," she said.

"Slave's obey orders, unless they want to be punished." My tone of voice was hard, Susie was resisting again. Surely by now she'd learned that it didn't matter what the order was, she was going to obey. Maybe there would be some pain first, or did she secretly like a bit of pain?"

Susie resisted again, I felt sorry for Willow, having to hold the cum in her mouth. "Willow, get my belt," I ordered. I watched Willow as she gracefully got off the bed and picked up my trousers, removed the belt from them and headed back to the bed. I took it in my hands and folded it in half, ready to use it on Susie.

I looked at Susie, she was transfixed, her eyes staring at the thick leather. I swished it in the air twice then looked at her. Susie opened her mouth then closed it, no words came out. She was terrified. And rightly so.

I raised the belt up, Susie tried to back away but there was nowhere for her to escape to, the bed was against the wall and she had backed into a corner. She covered her breasts with her hands but I grabbed her thin wrists and lifted her arms above her head, then brought the belt down hard into her soft, white chest, landing the belt across both breasts. Susie screamed in pain, I'm sure that some of the others heard her.

When she calmed down she begged me, or tried to, all she managed to say was "Please . . ." Please what? Please carry on? Please stop?

I lashed her again and she screamed in pain. "I'll do it, please, I'll do it."

I lashed her a third time. "You address me as Master," I said, "One more for forgetting." I gave her another, fat red stripes were starting to appear from where I'd hit her. Shit, my cock was twitching as well, I was enjoying this, maybe a little too much.

"I'm sorry master," she blubbed, "It won't happen again."

"Better not. OK girls, start kissing, but don't swallow a drop of cum."

The girls moved together, Willow's red hair mixing with Susie's blonde and they kissed, small tears were dripping down Susie's face. I made them kiss for five minutes before ordering all the cum into Susie's mouth.

"When I order you to swallow you will swallow and then thank me for tit whipping you and thank me for allowing you to swallow, understand?" Susie nodded, well, there wasn't much more she could do.

I made Susie kneel on the floor, Willow and I kissed then got dressed. I put the leash onto Susie's collar and made her walk on her hands and knees to the kitchen where Paul and Abi were in the kitchen eating breakfast.

"Hey, how was your night bud?"

"Fucking awesome," I replied.

"And Willow, how was your night? So Abi's the only girl in this apartment you've not fucked."

She smiled and kissed me, not speaking. Abi went a little red and looked down at Susie, who had stayed on all fours. Paul spun his seat round and lifted his legs, putting them on Susie's back.

"You don't mind do you?" he said, speaking to me and not Susie.

"Not at all Paul," I replied, "Help yourself. Abi,

you should put your feet up as well." Abi blushed even more as she turned and put her feet on Susie's back. Willow poured out coffee for the four of us at the table. As I looked down at Susie I spoke to her.

"You can swallow slave," I told her. Paul looked at me, I didn't answer until after Susie had spoken.

"Thank you for whipping my tits master to teach me a lesson. And thank you for allowing me to swallow you cum, it was delicious." She sounded utterly humiliated.

That was better than expected. Paul continued to stare at me, so I gave him a brief rundown of the morning's activities. When I'd finished I spoke to Susie again. "Are you a thirsty slave?" I asked her.

"Yes Master," she replied, still a little tone of defiance in her voice coming back.

I stood up and went to the percolator. I opened a cupboard and found a shallow bowl. I poured the coffee into it and then placed it under her face on the floor. She tried to lift one arm to pick up the bowl but I pushed it back.

"If you're thirsty, bow your head and drink from

the bowl slave."

She didn't answer, just lowered her head and started to lick at the hot brown liquid. I went and sat next to Willow and the four of us started to talk. Five minutes later Smokes came in and laughed when he saw how Susie was being used as a foot rest.

"Fuck me Jay, you've trained her well in one night," said Smokes as he lit his camel.

"Well, you just have to show her who the master is, don't you slave?"

This time she lifted her head from the bowl and spoke softly, "Yes Master."

"And why not tell Steve about your new favorite food?"

Steve looked at me, then Susie spoke from the floor. "Sir, this girl's new favorite food is cum sir. Sir, I'm sorry that I've never swallowed your cum sir." She paused before speaking again. "Please punish me sir."

Smokes let out a long exhale, the smoke filling the room. "Jay, mate, what the fuck did you do to her?"

I winked at him, "You'll never tell, will you slave?"

"No Master," she said sadly and put her head down to resume drinking her coffee. When we'd finished ours I stood up with Willow.

"Right, we're going for a bath." Susie moved, looking to crawl with us.

"No Slave, I've got a better idea." I reached into the pocket of my robe and pulled out a lipstick and a blindfold. I slipped the blindfold over Susie's head and ordered her to kneel. I tied the leash around a cupboard door and wrote on her ample chest – 'Free Blowjobs' then headed to the door, Willow following me.

"She's all yours Steve," I called as the door closed behind us. Willow laughed and grabbed my ass.

"You are naughty and I love the way you're controlling her."

I stopped walking. Now was the right moment, we were alone.

"Willow, I want you to call me sir and obey me,

when we are alone."

She swallowed and looked up at me – she's a good six inches shorter than me so had to look up. She took the half step to get up close to me and spoke softly.

"Yes sir," she said.

"Would you like to wear a collar like Susie's?"

"Very much so sir," she replied.

"Good, we'll shower and then walk into town, I've looked up a sex shop where we can buy you some things."

Willow went up on her toes and kissed me.

"I can't wait sir," she replied.

Behind us the kitchen door opened, Paul and Abi stepped out.

"Just leaving Smokes alone with Susi . . . slave," he said.

"Hey, it's an open offer. Abi, she's got a lot to

learn about eating pussy, but she's an enthusiastic learner, if you want to give her a try." Abi blushed, I suspected she'd be back to try later.

******

After we bathed and dressed I went to the kitchen to check on Susie, she was where I'd left her, she'd slouched to one side but straightened up as soon as I opened the door. I smiled and closed the door, leaving her there while we went shopping.

This was my first trip to a sex shop, I suspected it was Willow's as well. I expected it to be dirty and dingy, hidden away on a back street, staffed by a dirty old man with stained nails and a shitty attempt at a beard. Nothing could be further from my expectation. When we went in I was pleasantly surprised, the place was brightly lit and cavernous – honestly, it must have been 250 feet from the front to the back of the store. And the staff, oh my god the staff, I could have come in just to look at the staff. There must have been a dozen women working there, all in their early to late 20's, all wearing bright red lingerie, push up bras, stocking and suspenders with matching red high heel shoes. Fuck, I've lived here for six years, why oh why have I never been in here before?

We walked up and down, the store was arranged

by genre, so lingerie was by the door, sex toys were down one wall, books in one area. A sign at the back pointed to upstairs, this was marked 'for him'. Maybe later. I picked up a basket and more than one outfit for Willow. I'd get her to try them on later, after we found the BDSM section.

We must have looked lost, behind me I heard a woman ask "Are you looking for something in particular sir?" We turned round, her name lapel was pinned to her bra. She was about 28, five foot six or seven, large breasts, flat stomach and great legs. I swallowed, my voice failed me, I mean come on, when you buy a suit the man selling it calls you sir, but when it's a scantily clad woman with long blonde hair and big tits I couldn't help but think about fucking her. I bet guys hit on her all the time. Willow came to my rescue.

"Hi Lucy," she said, "We're looking for BDSM gear."

"No problem," Lucy replied, "Come with me, it's in the basement." Lucy gave a half laugh and added, "Or dungeon, if you want to think of it that way." We followed Lucy, we'd missed the sign pointing to the basement – probably as we were looking in awe at the displays and staff. As Lucy went down the stairs Willow pinched my ass.

"Nice view isn't it sir?" She wasn't wrong.

In the basement Lucy paused to allow us to look around for a moment. "Would you like me to help you or would you like to look on your own?"

"Please, can you help us Lucy?" I said, my voice coming back, "I'm Jay, this is Willow." Lucy nodded to us both.

"So Jay, what are you looking for?"

I took a deep breath, "To be honest Lucy, I'm not 100% sure, we've recently started experimenting with BDSM and we're looking to take it to the next stage."

"No problem," Lucy said, smiling, "You've come to the right place." I looked round again, she wasn't wrong, I could see everything I'd ever heard of, everything I'd ever imagined and a shit load of stuff that I had no idea what it was. Shopping was going to be fun.

"So, where shall we start?" asked Lucy?

"How about collars and leashes?" I suggested.

"Sure, follow me folks." We walked a short distance to an aisle that had nothing but collars on it, some loose, some in packs with leashes or wrist/ankle cuffs. I didn't know where to start.

"So," said Lucy, "Who's the submissive?"

Fuck, I hadn't thought about that. Willow spoke. "I am."

"Great, there's a better choice for women anyway. What's your budget?"

"Doesn't matter," I said to Lucy.

"Are you sure? Some of these collars are pretty expensive." She bent down and picked one up. "Take this for example," she added, handing it to me, "Made of silver, this would set you back about $420 with tax, or if you're just starting out we've got this one, more like $20", she said handing me a thin leather collar. It looked cheap.

"Somewhere in between. Say $50 to $100?"

Lucy spent the next 20 minutes showing us collars and explaining the differences, from soft leather that was easier to wear, to thick leather ones that barely moved – she called them posture collars that would force Willow to hold her head in once position. Lucy pointed out that these wouldn't be very comfortable and not suitable for long term use. She showed us steel collars, thin subtle ones that could be passed off as chokers. In the end we settled on two, one was stiff leather, about two inches thick with rings front and back, that could be padlocked in place. The other was thin leather with a love heart on it that Willow wanted to wear day to day.

We spent almost two hours with Lucy, in addition to the collars we picked up cuffs, floggers, gags, whips, nipple clamps, sex toys – the list went on and on. When we'd shopped out I asked if Willow could try on the outfits.

"Of course," said Lucy, "The changing rooms are over here." Willow went in and put on a black lingerie set and came out.

"She looks incredible Jay," said Lucy, "You're a very lucky man." She was right, I am. "Are you going to try the collar on her?" Good idea.

I picked the collar out of the basket and put it round Willow's neck. Lucy lifted her long red hair out of the way and I put the hook into place, fastening it on her neck. Lucy offered me the padlock and I locked the collar in place.

"How does that feel Willow?" asked Lucy. Willow put her hands onto the collar and felt it.

"Incredible," she replied.

"Want to try more on her Jay?" asked Lucy.

"Sure." There were about a dozen people walking round the basement, several had stopped to watch Lucy and I dress Willow. Lucy picked a ball gag out of the basket and inserted it into Willow's mouth. Willow opened wide and took the ball behind her teeth as Lucy fastened it behind Willow's head. She asked Willow if it was OK and Willow nodded.

"First time?" Willow nodded. Lucy turned to me, "Don't leave it in for too long, it makes your jaw very sore, you have to get used to it."

"Have you worn one then Lucy?" Fuck, I was flirting with Lucy stood in front of my girlfriend.

"Oh yes," she replied with a wide grin on her face, "I've worn one overnight – if you're planning on that though get one with a hole in it, just in case her nose gets blocked overnight – you don't want her to suffocate do you?" I nodded, God no I don't want her to die. Good to know!

Lucy picked out the wrist cuffs and Willow extended her arms. Lucy fitted them onto Willow, then pushed Willow's hands behind her back and locked them together. When Lucy came back in front of Willow she ran her hands over Willow's breasts. This was very sensual, Lucy was going above and beyond.

"Shall we try some nipple clamps on your slave Jay?" I nodded, this was very erotic. Lucy picked up the clamps. I folded my arms to watch. Lucy put her left hand onto Willow' lacy bra and pulled at it, she put her right hand inside the bra and pulled her breast out. I looked round, no one was shopping now, everyone was watching the show. I looked at Willow's eyes gauging her reaction, she looked like she was enjoying being played with. Lucy repeated the maneuver on her other breast, freeing it from it's holder. Lucy then played with one of Willow's nipples, quickly it sprang erect and Lucy put the clamp on.

"Ow," said Willow through her gag.

Lucy smiled, "It's supposed to hurt slave, that's the point." Lucy showed me how to adapt the spring, causing Willow more or less pain. She then put the other on onto her other nipple. Lucy looked at Willow, then leaned in and kissed her through the gag. I had to put my hands down my pants now to adjust my cock, it was rock hard.

"One final thing for today," said Lucy. She picked up the blindfold and slipped it over Willow's head. She looked at me and picked the leash out of the basket. Lucy handed it to me, "She's your property Jay, you should leash her."

I took the leash and clipped it onto the collar. Willow couldn't see a thing, she was completely under my control. I looked at Lucy.

"Do you want some sex toys as well for her Jay?"

"Good idea," I replied, this was going to be a very expensive shopping trip but what the hell? Lucy picked up Willow's clothes and started to walk slowly to the stairs. I followed her, carrying the basket and pulling on the leash. I kept it short so I could control Willow easily. As we walked people in the store shouted their encouragement and thanks for what they'd seen.

I had to help Willow up the stairs. As we got onto the main floor the place fell silent as we walked to the sex toys section. Lucy suggested a re-mote controlled vibrator, some love eggs and anal beads. Her final suggestion was a book on rope bondage for beginners.

The bill came to almost $1,400, but worth every cent. After I paid I looked at Lucy, I don't know what came over me as I put my credit card back in my wallet, I've never been confident round women but I had to do this. I handed her my business card, Lucy looked at it.

"If you want to play with Willow and me some-time give me a call. We're having a party tonight if you want to come?"

Lucy smiled coyly, "I can't come tonight Jay, but I will call you some time? Maybe next Friday after work?"

"Call me mid-week and we can talk. We play cards on a Friday night, but you'd be welcome. It's not your normal game of cards."

"Sounds interesting," she said, "I'll call you later."

We turned to leave. "Are you forgetting some-thing Jay?" Lucy called out. I looked at her. Fuck, she was holding Willow's clothes. I'd been about to lead Willow out into the street semi naked, gagged and bound. I'd have been arrested within

10 minutes. Lucy helped me remove the gag and unlock the handcuffs. At her suggestion we left it at that and put Willow's coat on to walk her back to the apartment. Naturally I made Willow carry the bags, I just pulled her leash.

We got several stares and comments as we walked back to the apartment but I didn't care. Once inside the stairwell I removed Willow's collar, I wasn't ready for the others to see slave Willow. Well, not just yet anyway. I put the love heart choker on her instead. Once inside Willow took the bags to our room and I went to the kitchen, opened the fridge and pulled out a couple of coke zeros for us. I looked round, I'd expected to see Susie where I'd left her, but she wasn't there.

I went to the living room, Willow was coming the other way and we went in together. Smokes was in there, watching the TV. He was smoking, un-usual, he doesn't normally smoke in there but it's his apartment, we can hardly stop him. Susie was kneeling next to him.

"How was your morning?" asked Steve.

"Awesome, and you?"

"Couldn't be better. Two blowjobs from Slave

here, which is two more than I got in the last year, isn't it?" Susie didn't speak. We sat down and chatted as Steve puffed away. When there was a half inch of ash on the end of his cigarette I noticed there wasn't an ashtray.

"Go get an ashtray slave," I ordered.

"No need," said Steve. Susie stayed where she was and he moved the cigarette towards her. Susie leaned her head back and opened her mouth wide, Steve tapped the camel against her teeth and the ash fell into her open mouth. As he moved it away Susie closed her mouth and swallowed the ash, coughing a little.

"Check out her tits Jay, I had to persuade her to be my ashtray." I looked at her tits, there were a dozen stripes where she'd been hit. Well, come Monday Susie would either be his slave or he'd be single. There was no going back for him now. I looked at Willow, she was shocked, as to be honest, was I. We talked for a moment, then left. I didn't want to see what Steve did with the filter when he got to the end.

In our room Willow said. "I'm excited to submit to you sir, but just to let you know that's a step too far."

"I agree, I'll never make you do that Willow. Never. In fact, do you want a safe word – in case I go too far?"

"Yes please sir. How about 'Ghostbusters'?" I laughed, who you gonna call?

******

We went out for lunch then walked round the harbor, I left Susie with Steve. I'd get her back for the night. The party would start at eightish and would be in full swing by ten. We needed beer so Paul and I went to Costco in his car and we loaded up, leavings Jon and Steve to get the girls to clean and tidy. When we got back we unloaded and filled the fridge, then we all went out for something to eat. In the restaurant I ordered for Willow and Susie, not even allowing them to look at the menu. I was enjoying controlling them both.

We got back just before eight, it was time to introduce Susie to her role for the night. As soon as we got into the apartment I ordered her to strip and she obeyed. She was learning fast. I clipped the leash onto her collar, then Steve and I took her to the box room. In the afternoon he'd constructed what he'd said he would, a wooden box, about four feet high and two feet wide and two feet deep. On the front was written 'Free Blowjob'. Steve had built a Glory Hole. Susie worked it out quickly, her face was clouded with fear and she tried to back away.

"You're doing this slave," I told her, "You can either get in there now, or I can whip you until you beg to get in. Your choice."

Poor Susie, she stopped resisting then looked at us both. Very quietly she said, "Please put me in the glory hole master." I looked at Steve, we smiled at each other. Clearly the fear of another whipping was working on her. Steve took the lid off and we lifted her in. Susie went to kneel down, when I ordered her to stand. I took off the leather collar and instead put on an electric shock collar. Susie didn't know what it was so I showed her by pressing the button. She jumped in pain and shrieked as it shocked her.

"See, if your 'customers' don't think you are performing they can 'encourage' you try harder."

Steve threw a couple of cushions in for her to kneel on, she'd be in there for many hours, didn't want her to be too uncomfortable. We put the lid on and stood a TV on top of the box and screwed the lid down. The TV was linked to a night camera inside the box so people could see who was servicing their cocks. We were pleased with our handiwork.

The hole in the front of the box was just over three inches in diameter, big enough to get any-one's cock through but there would be no chance of a hand getting in. Likewise the box was tight enough that Susie would only be able to use her mouth and hands to get guys off, she wouldn't be able to turn round so that they could use her pussy or ass. Nope, oral only for Susie.

As a final touch Steve had put a pen and paper on top of the box, with a request that everyone that made use of the blow job facility sign in – he didn't want names, just a count of the cocks that she had serviced and a score out of 10. He warned Susie that she'd better not get worse over the course of the night.

I turned to leave when I heard a muffled scream from inside the box. I turned back to look, Steve was standing in front of the box, the shock collar control box in hand, his body jammed up against the box. I laughed, he was having a trial run. On the TV/monitor I could see Susie writhing as Steve shocked her.

By the way this wasn't a BDSM themed party, just your normal student drunken mess. Susie was the only difference to any other party we'd ever held. But it was going to make it a popular one.

The party passed like any other, we had to eject a few people but other than that we had dancing in the living room, some people played cards in the dining room and the best conversation was in the kitchen. Willow loves to dance, me not so much so we didn't see a lot of each other. Every time I checked on the box room there was a queue of guys waiting outside. Poor Susie, she couldn't have been having a great time. Her mouth must have been painful from being forced open all night.

The gathering wound down by two am and we ejected the stragglers by two thirty. Steve and I went to the box room to extract Susie, as we lifted her out we could see what a mess she was in. Her makeup was streaked and smeared, her body and hair covered in sperm. Steve checked the sheet, mostly eights and nines out of ten. He picked up the control for the shock collar and pressed it, nothing happened. Shit, the batteries had been worn down to nothing. Susie was shaking so we helped carry her to the kitchen.

Willow got her a drink and some food to eat which she accepted gratefully. We left her on the floor, eating from a bowl while we tidied up. I say we tidied up, all us boys sat down and talked while Willow, Abi and Mia cleaned up. At one point Willow came in with a bar of soap. She ordered Susie to her knees and pushed the soap into Susie's mouth, ordering her to bite down on it.

I looked at Willow quizzically.

"Well, she's had so much cock and sperm in her slut mouth I want it nice and clean before it goes anywhere near me tonight. Don't you?"

I looked down at Susie, foam was forming round her mouth where her spit was escaping. She was coughing and spluttering.

"Make sure that doesn't come out until I remove it slut," said Willow turning to leave. As she did we all laughed. Willow had a dirty, dominant streak in her.

When the apartment was clean enough (it would need a further clean tomorrow) the girls came in and we all went off to our rooms, I rode Susie back to mine, soap still in her mouth, with Willow following. As soon as we got there I ordered Susie to the bathroom, on her hands and knees to remove the soap which had been in her mouth for over 20 minutes or so and clean her teeth. As much as I enjoyed seeing Susie humiliated like this I didn't want to taste the soap on her mouth.

When she came back I ordered both girls to kneel on the floor, legs wide apart.

"Is your mouth clean slave?" I asked her.

"I, I think so master," she replied, "I cleaned my teeth twice."

"Willow, kiss her and see what you think."

"Yes sir," replied Willow and the girls turned to face each other and they kissed for a few seconds. I don't think I could ever get bored of watching Willow kiss another woman. There's just something about sexy lesbians, especially when they are submissive to you.

When they broke off Willow said "Sir, there is a faint taste of soap on the slave's mouth."

My first thought was to punish her, by the way that Susie moved slowly backwards it was clear she was thinking the same way. But it wouldn't be fair to do that, she'd clearly tried her best and let's be honest, that bar of soap had been in her mouth for over 20 minutes, she'd done well to get it as clean as she had.

"OK slave," I said, "Let's see what you learned in that box. Think you can get more down your throat?"

"I think so master, I had lots of practice in there tonight."

I opened my legs and Susie moved closer, she knew what to do. Her jaw must have been pretty sore, I have no idea how many guys she'd blown but it must have been 20 plus. A bit like being gagged for five hours, just with sperm as well.

I lay back and Susie started to lick my cock. She opened wide and took me into her mouth, last time she'd managed only a couple of inches, this time she was like a seasoned pro and she managed to get all but the last inch in before she gagged. I pulled her hair, lifting her off my cock.

"You've got a lot better at that slave."

"Thank you master, I have been practicing." Shit, that was a half-smile she gave me.

"Did you enjoying sucking all those cocks slave?"

She didn't reply straight away, she blushed and quietly said, "Yes sir." Fuck, was she turning into a real slave, or just pleased to suck cock? I pushed her back, getting her back to work on my shaft. Willow had stayed on the floor, watching. Tempting though it was to have her watch me fuck Susie I had to get real, the chance to fuck two girls at the same time doesn't come along that frequently.

"Get up here Willow," I ordered her.

Willow didn't speak, she just stood up and got onto the bed next to me. I turned to face her and we kissed, our legs hanging over the bed edge.

"Eat Willow," I ordered, "And wank me."

Susie didn't speak, she just moved and started to suck on Willow's cunt and wank me slowly. An idea was forming in my mind. I ordered Susie to play with her cunt as well, she should keep all three of us entertained.

I made Susie continue like this for a few minutes as Willow and I kissed, it was very erotic. When I was happy that Willow was wet enough I pushed her away and ordered Susie up onto the bed, legs on the floor, spread wide, face down, ass & cunt showing. Then I got Willow to lie on top of her, also face down. I stood up and pushed my cock into Willow first, she gasped in delight as I pounded her pussy, my balls underneath banging against Susie.

After a couple of minutes I pulled out of Willow and straight into Susie, I wanted to fuck her ass but I remembered Mia's words, she'd need proper lubrication, so I just made use of her cunt. After a couple of swaps I made the girls move, getting Willow on her back with Susie on top, their breasts pushing together, kissing passionately.

I moved back and forth between their cunts, taking turns, using one hole then the other. Willow was trying harder, her cunt was tighter and wetter than Susie. I couldn't take much more of this and soon I cried out in delight. I pulled out of Susie and wanked myself, Willow and Susie quickly got off each other and onto the floor, they put their faces together, mouths open as I came, shooting cum all over their pretty faces.

When I stopped cumming Susie surprised me by leaning forward and taking me back into her mouth to clean me, Willow moved to lick my balls. After a while I pulled out and the girls licked the sticky white cum off each other's faces, when it was all gone they continued to kiss, sharing my load.

I watched until I'd had enough, then ordered them to swallow and stop. We all used the bathroom, I considered making them get in the shower cubicle and making them drink my piss, but that might well be too far for Willow – fuck I didn't want to lose her.

In bed I allowed them to swallow, then told Susie to take my cock into her mouth and hold it there all night. She moved, then looked at me.

"Master, am I allowed to sleep tonight?"

I stroked her soft hair. "Of course you are slave." Susie smiled, then I added, "But if I wake up and my cock isn't in your mouth you're in for a severe punishment." Susie was visibly shocked, she was weighing up her options, then she spoke.

"No sleep for me tonight then Master." She paused and then added, "Can I take it out once in a while Master so I can swallow?" That was fair enough and I told her so.

I kissed Willow and we went to sleep, leaving my cock buried in Susie's face. Willow was out in seconds, it took me a long time to drop off, having your cocked sucked makes it tricky to fall asleep.

SUNDAY APRIL 12TH

We woke late, Willow was lying next to me, I moved a little and could feel Susie respond, her mouth was still wrapped round my cock. I could feel her warm breath on my balls. I doubt she'd slept at all, she would have been terrified of the consequences of me waking and my dick wasn't in her mouth.

I put my hands onto Susie's head, my cock was already growing in her mouth. I took handfuls of her hair and started to push her up and down, she quickly got the idea and started to suck. She'd come a long way in 36 hours.

I twisted slightly to face Willow, then grabbed one of her nipples in my fingers and twisted it gently, the resulting pain woke her up. She rolled onto her side, then up onto one elbow and we started to kiss. I had planned to fuck them both again, but this just seemed too perfect a way to wake up, kissing the woman I loved and having my cock sucked by another. And the best part? The woman I loved was up for it.

It wasn't long before I felt my balls tightening, Susie was cupping them and she felt it too, she squeezed gently and I started to cum, I flopped back on the bed as I shot my load into Susie's mouth. She'd learned a lot, she didn't pull away, just pushed her head down as far as she could, catching it all in her mouth. When I finished cumming she didn't pull off either, just put her head on my chest and lay there, my cock still buried in her mouth.

Willow and I talked about Susie the slave, then we laughed. I threw the covers off and Willow grabbed Susie's hair, pulling her off.

"Still got all you master's cum slave?" Susie nodded by way of reply. "Good girl," Willow added. I loved the look of utter humiliation that came over Susie when Willow said that, it must have been degrading for her to be told that by another woman, a slave and yet still her superior. "Now go and get both of us a coffee."

Susie backed off the bed and stood up. "Crawl bitch," yelled Willow. Instantly Susie dropped to her hands and knees and crawled out of the room.

It took her 10 minutes to come back, I was in half a mind to going to look for her when the door opened. Then I worked out why she was taking so long, a cup appeared, then another. Then in crawled Susie, she picked up one cup and moved it three feet, then the other and she crawled a little more. Willow and I laughed again.

Willow jumped off the bed and picked the coffee up and gave one to me.

"Your coffee sir," she said and we started to drink it. I looked over a Susie, she was kneeling, legs apart, hands on her thighs as she'd been trained. I couldn't help smiling.

When we'd drunk up we went to the bathroom, I had Susie hold my dick as I pissed in the toilet bowl, she looked disgusted with herself, then we showered, I stood there, enjoying the warm water cascading over my body as the two girls cleaned me (I'd recommend this to anyone by the way). We dressed and went to the kitchen were everyone else was.

I made Susie open her mouth wide to show my cum, then allowed her to swallow. She thanked me as she'd been trained and we all laughed, then discussed what we'd do that day, Susie serving us coffee and cookies.

7 of us left the apartment for brunch that day, Susie of course stayed behind to clean up. We were out until midafternoon, when we finally got home the apartment was clean. Susie had had a bath or a shower and she was back to her stunning best. We spent the afternoon making her perform tasks, like a performing dog. We raced her, sitting on her back and riding her up and down the long corridor.

Later I got my ropes and book on bondage and we spent the early evening tying and retying Susie in different positions. I think my favorite was when Jon tied a thin rope round her huge tits, pulling them tighter and tighter until we ran out of cord. I tied a second rope to the one holding her tits down then tied the end of that to her toes, forcing her to bend double, ass and cunt on display. We secured her arms behind her back and put a bag over her head. Jon, Smokes and I then fucked her in turn, she had to guess who was using her pussy – if she guessed wrong she got a stroke from the cane. I could see that Paul wanted to join in, but he didn't know how to ask Abi.

In the evening we went out for something to eat, we took Susie but I made her leave her collar on. It was only the threat of taking her out in a bikini and still leaving the collar on that made her agree to wear it in public. It would be good for her. She got a lot of attention in the restaurant and then in the bar later. It's not every day you see a collared, leashed woman in public.

When we got home I handed her leash to Smokes.

"Her last night as a slave Steve, you should have her."

"Really?" I looked at Susie, all the fight was out of her, once more she was being traded as a piece of meat.

"Sure."

I watched him walk away. It would probably be the last night he ever had with her.

Willow and I went into our room, I removed her choker and put on her slave collar. She breathed deeply as I put it on.

"You like wearing this, don't you?"

"No sir, I love wearing your collar. Hopefully one day you'll parade me like you did with Susie."

One day I would. We were both pretty tired after the late party so we just went to bed and slept.

MONDAY
APRIL 13TH

I could cheerfully have smashed the alarm clock that morning but work comes first. I got up and showered, Willow was dressed when I came in, her slave collar removed and choker back on.

"It's not as good sir," she said as I closed the door and we went to the kitchen for breakfast. It was just before eight. Everyone else was sat round the table, Susie kneeling at Smoke's side, he was holding her leash. As I walked in he handed it to me and took control of her for the last five minutes.

When the clock ticked over to eight I reached into my pocket and removed the padlock from the collar and took it off. I handed it to Smokes and looked at Susie.

"You're free now Susie, free to do whatever you want."

Susie looked up and me and crawled to Smokes. I expected her to hit him, to scream, to announce that it was all over. Instead she just knelt in front of him.

"Sure?" Smokes asked?

"Yes," she replied. Smokes took the collar and put it back on her neck. I looked at Willow and smiled. Susie was now making a choice, she was becoming Smoke's property.

"Understand that from this moment forth you have no rights what so ever," Smokes told Susie, "I own you and can do what I want with you. You cannot say no. You cannot terminate this agreement, ever.

"I understand and accept your collar willingly Master," she replied.

Holy fuck, Mia was a slave, Susie was a slave, Willow was a slave (albeit a secret one). What about Abi? Would she be a slave?

We set off for work just after that, leaving the girls behind.

******

"But why not?" asked Willow, "Why will you not make my slave status known to the others?"

"Not yet," I said, "And Willow, two things. One, you do not question my decisions. And two, you address me as sir, understand?"

"Yes sir."

"Now take my belt off, stand up and bend over. 12 strokes to your ass for forgetting to call me sir and another 12 for questioning me."

Willow swallowed as she stood up. This was her first real punishment.

"Yes sir."

When she was in position I raised up the belt and brought it down into her pale white skin. She screamed in pain as I brought the belt down hard on to her. I smiled, 23 more to go, then I'd fuck her in that position.

FRIDAY APRIL 17TH

8:25pm, we'd just sat down to play poker.

"So, what's the game going to be?"

Just then the door bell rang, as I expected.

"Willow," I said, "Can you get that please?" Everyone else looked at me.

"Expecting someone are you?"

I just raised my eyebrows and grinned, ignoring the question. We talked as I shuffled the cards, we heard Willow come back into the apartment and then walk down the corridor, past the dining room. I acted like this was expected, as it was. It was another 10 minutes before Willow came back. The door opened and she came in, wearing a matching bra/panties set in black. She had a ball gag in her mouth, her hands were cuffed behind her back. Paul opened his mouth to speak, then closed it as Lucy, from the sex shop came in. She was dressed just like Willow, right down to the gag. Both of them came and stood behind me.

I reached under the table and pulled out a bag, I pulled two collars out of the bag and turned to face my girls. I put one on Lucy first, then the second on Willow.

"Gentlemen, this is Lucy," I said, gesturing to the stunning blonde behind me, "and she's joining us for the game. She will be the winner's slave for the weekend. Willow, on the other hand, is my slave now, aren't you Willow?"

Willow nodded and made a reasonable attempt at "Yes sir."

Smokes spoke first, "Susie, strip to your underwear."

"Yes Master," she said.

Jon was next. He ordered Mia to get her collar and strip to the same level. Abi was last, unasked she removed her clothes and whispered in Pauls' ear.

"Fuck yes," he said, "Abi has just asked to be my slave. I've agreed to take her on." We all laughed.

"So," I said, "Tonight I thought we could do something a little different. How about we all start with $20,000 and when someone runs out of money the winner picks a girl for the night. Then we reset the money and play again until we've had five winners."

So at least one guy was going to end up with two girls. Lucy would go first, there was no doubt about that. New pussy, who wouldn't want it?

Six weeks ago we'd all been so pissed off when Susie forgot her fake ID. Now it seemed like the best mistake anyone had ever made.

AFTERWORD

Thank you for reading this book. I really hope you enjoyed reading it as much as I enjoyed writing it.

If you did enjoy it please leave a review or star rating on Amazon (even an anonymous rating would be wonderful), or do please get in touch, I love hearing from people who read my books.

Paige
xx

https://www.amazon.com/author/paige.bond

paige.bond.author@gmail.com

ABOUT THE AUTHOR

Paige Bond

I was born in the late 90's and I've been fascinated by BDSM, particularly female submission for as long as I can remember. My stories are based on my own real-life experiences, or things that I fantasize about happening to me. I write as frequently as I can, concentrating on longer books - if you find something you like please let me know.

Follow me on twitter
https://twitter.com/PaigeBondAuthor

Check out my other books on Amazon
https://www.amazon.com/author/paige.bond

Email me - I love getting feedback
paige.bond.author@gmail.com

Ask me a question!
Ask me a question https://curiouscat.qa/Paige-BondAuthor

PRAISE FOR AUTHOR

[Blackmailed]

I couldn't put this book down for a second even though it is a little twisted at some points I loved it.

- GEORGINA

[5 Days in San Fransico]

This is the first time I've bothered to pen a review, and the first time I've read this author. I've read quite a few ponygirl/ hucow stories and other sort of dom/sub stories. To date it is the best and I will most certainly be revisiting the world of this writer. The mix of what is realistic and what is oft written about, but not realistic is nicely balanced and flows well. I give

- JONEL

[5 Days in San Fransico]

Well written. Ideas were nicely executed. Characters were real. Details well imaged. Will read more by this author. Folsom street fair. Described well.

- LORIN

[Pony Girl Ranch : Fire and Flame]

I can't wait to hear more a great story

- GARY

BOOKS BY THIS AUTHOR

5 Days In San Francisco

India is a young English girl crossing America after leaving University. She's broke and looking for somewhere to stay in San Francisco for 5 nights. Mason's in his mid 30s and recently single looking for some fun. They meet on Tinder and strike up a 5 day romance. India wants to experience San Francisco's alternative scene.

Over the course of their 5 days together Mason shows her the best that San Fran has to offer, she stars in a porn film shoot, they attend a BDSM orgy and the Folsom Street Fair, where India is paraded round the streets naked.

"Are you hungry? Shall we get something to eat?"

"Yes please sir, I've not eaten since yesterday lunch," she replied, then in a seductive tone she added, "and what you have planned for later sir?"

Mason smiled and reached into his bag. He took out a thin steel collar with a ring at the front. He unlocked it and opened it, moving the device towards India's neck. She half stepped back, looking around nervously.

"Don't worry, this is San Francisco. We're a couple of blocks from Fulsom Street. No one will care. Where we're going for breakfast I doubt anyone will even notice – hell, they might say that you're underdressed."

He continued to smile and after a moment she nodded.

"Have you ever worn one before?" he asked.

"No sir," she replied, "but I've often thought about it."

Pony Girl Ranch : Fire And Flame

Lisa is stuck in a dead end job, living with an abusive boyfriend. Her only escape from her dreary life is 2 afternoons a week working at a stables. Lisa is envious of the horses, of the pampered life that they lead. One day she's browsing porn and comes across a video that changes her life : Pony Girl porn. Lisa becomes obsessed with pony girl porn and contacts Rachel who trains pony girls. Before long she signs up for a pony girl trial, 13 weeks living and working as a pony girl, devoid of human rights, devoid of human speech.

Rachel extended a hand on Lisa's chin and raised her head up slightly.

"Is there anything you want to ask me Lisa?"

Lisa thought for a while. "Have you ever been a pony girl?"

Rachel laughed, "Of course. Maybe seven or eight years ago? I did a one week taster, then came back for the full 13 weeks you're about to experience. I didn't really want to be pony, I wanted to be a trainer. But Travis won't allow any trainers who've not experienced what it's like to be a pony."

"What's it like?" asked Lisa. Her face was full of desire about being a pony.

"It's hard work, don't be fooled for a moment. It's also incredible, you'll drive men – and women – wild with desire." Lisa smiled at that, she found it hard to believe that she could drive anyone wild with desire, six months of Adam putting her down had left a mark on her confidence. Rachel could see the doubt.

"You will, you'll lose weight, get more defined, and with your hair," Rachel added, running her hands through Lisa's long red hair, "Don't doubt yourself Lisa, everyone will want to fuck you."

"Do I get any choice in who fucks me?"

"No."

Lisa was taken aback at Rachel's abruptness. She thought for a moment. "What happens at the end of the 13 weeks?"

"You'll move into the house for two weeks. I'm guessing you don't have any ties to here, so will you let your accommodation slide?" Lisa nodded. "In those two weeks we'll help you find somewhere to live, set you up with interviews, jobs if that's what you want. And generally get you used to be being a human again." Rachel smiled at Lisa. "Any more questions?"

"No."

A Pony For Christmas (And Other Stories)

In this exciting collection of Pony Girl stories you'll meet some people from Pony Girl Ranch : Fire and Flame as well as new characters and situations. This bumper collection is over 55,000 words with 10 stories, including novella 'A Pony Girl for Christmas', the direct sequel to Fire and Flame.

Daddy's Pony Girl
Alone in the house after her return from University Paula discovers a locked trunk. When she breaks into it she finds all kind of pony girl equipment which she decides to experiment with before her Daddy gets home.

My First Pony
What do you buy your son for his 21st birthday when he already has everything? Rolex - he's got several. Supercar? Name one he doesn't have. One thing he doesn't have is a Pony Girl, and who wouldn't want one for their 21st?

The Blacksmith's Tale
All ponies need to be shod, but where do you find someone who'll shod a pony girl? When Steve gets a request from a very unusual client he goes to work on the ranch for a week, where he learns that not all ponies have 4 legs.

Read all of these and 7 more in this bumper collection.

Blackmailed

Sarah is a young, naive girl who lives with her step-father. She thinks it will be exciting to offer herself to an unknown man to obey his orders and perform his tasks while she is filmed, he will then use the film to blackmail her to perform more and more degrading tasks. Soon, Sarah finds herself playing a game in which she is no longer in control and afraid of the consequences if she doesn't obey. Over the months her blackmailer takes total control of Sarah's life, making her perform more degrading and disgusting acts, each one more demeaning than the last.

Sarah,

Your next task is simple. On Friday night you are to be at the north entrance of the park near your house at eight pm. There you will strip naked (you may wear shoes if you want). You will place your hands behind your back and walk to the south entrance. Once there you will sit on the bench for two minutes before walking back to the north entrance. You may not dress until eight thirty pm. You must stay on the path at all times. I will be watching you at some point.

Your Master

Printed in Great Britain
by Amazon

82527594R00159